RESTORING REBECCA

*A story of traumatic stress, caregiving,
and the unmasking of a superhero*

CHRISTOPHER MARCHAND

Outskirts Press, Inc.
Denver, Colorado

Restoring Rebecca
A story of traumatic stress, caregiving, and the unmasking of a superhero

Thanks to Brenda Peters for the cover design photography and to Mandy Reimer and "Max" (the golden retriever) Neufeld for modeling.

Outskirts Press, Inc.
http://www.outskirtspress.com

ISBN: 978-1-4327-2949-3

Outskirts Press and the "OP" logo are trademarks belonging to Outskirts Press, Inc.

PRINTED IN THE UNITED STATES OF AMERICA

~ For Justin and Brianna ~

For the longest time there was nothing more important to me than finding ways to care for the people and the animals in my life. Caring for others is as natural to me as breathing or eating might be to someone else. It's just what I love to do. I guess that's why I was so surprised to find out that caring for others could make me sick. That still sounds a bit weird to say and maybe it seems strange to read. After you're done reading my story, I hope you'll understand what I mean. My name is Rebecca and I'm a character created from the real lives of people who have shared their stories of caring with the author. Although I'm not a real person, you'll recognize that the life situations I face in this story are very real. Everyday, caring people just like me take the time to listen to painful and sometimes unbelievably graphic stories of suffering experienced by their closest friends. I guess sometimes we feel safer talking to friends about painful things in our lives. We connect better with people who already know us and care for us, but even then it can be hard to talk about things like abuse, addiction, violence, depression, rape, or cutting. We all know that you don't have to look far to find friends who struggle with these kinds of things and, if you're anything like me, you have a way of sensing needs, even before you hear the story. You look into their eyes and you just know; this person needs to talk.

I've had to learn that sensing needs and feeling another person's pain is both a good thing and a bad thing. That's still hard for me to admit and it's ok if it sounds odd to you. I used to believe that it was selfish to think about my own feelings, but then I don't want to give too much of the story away. I had to learn that caring for other people will affect me and my relationships with those I love. It's so weird; one day it just hits you. All of a sudden you feel so empty and hollow, like you're all cared out, with nothing left to give. You want to cry, but your body feels so numb that you can't even squeeze out a tear. After I heard Zach's story, I just couldn't focus. It was like I was walking around in a dream. And then there was Amy's pain, and Clifton's accident, and Alisa's secret; I felt overwhelmed. As you'll see, I needed Dr. Anderson to help me understand that I wouldn't be any help to my friends if I didn't find a way to refill my empty cup. If you love to care for others, then this story is for you. I hope it will make you cry and laugh and challenge you to think about the way you care for yourself as you care for the people you love.

If you'd like, you can check out the back section of the book before beginning to read. You'll find some questions to help you think about what's happening in the story and you'll see a chart listing many of the things that I experience during my week. I hope you enjoy my story and I hope it helps you to learn to love the people in your life even better than you already do!

Your Friend,
Rebecca

TABLE OF CONTENTS

Part III: Change

PART 1

CARING FOR FRIENDS IN PAIN

~ 1 UNWANTED GUEST ~

Spring felt like a visit from an old friend after the friend you didn't really like had stayed about six months too long. The cold took a hold of Winnipeg in mid-October, and hung on like a puppy on a chew toy until the end of March. It's funny how the month of June can revive you after months of living in a deep freeze. It was Monday morning and warm summer sunshine was on his mind, as sixteen-year-old Zach tossed his winter coat on the bed, choosing his favorite hooded sweater instead. "Finally," he said to himself out loud, not bothering to hide an uncharacteristic smile and pulling on his favorite hooded sweater.

"Zach honey, could you see who's at the door? I've got to finish this hair or I'm going to be late, and I can't be late again," Zach's mom yelled over the whine of the blow dryer. She had finally landed a job with a cleaning company in Winnipeg. It was good to see his mom more like her old self, Zach thought, as he started toward the living room and to the front door of their tiny apartment. It had been almost a year since the divorce and during that time Zach had watched helplessly as his strong, capable mother had deteriorated into a bed-ridden mess. But he'd never given up. He was smart enough to know that she was still in there, somewhere, lost behind the tears and the melancholy. A violent alcoholic husband had ruined her marriage, her dreams, and nearly killed one of her sons.

Zach had heard stories of drunks who were the life of the party, crazies who would load up on drinks, play the court jester, make a fool of themselves, and pass out. No harm done, or so he was told. His dad was the other kind of drunk - the kind who used alcohol to make up for his lack of courage. The kind of drunk who had ruled his wife, and his son, with an iron fist, demanding perfection and obedience, and punishing the slightest mistake with humiliation and pain. The kind of drunk who consumed not just alcohol, but people and joy and space and even the air in a room with his whiskey stench and his putrid excuses for his behaviour. And what excuse could there possibly be for his dad's violence toward him? The answer was simple: Clifton. It was true that Zach hated his father's drinking and the humiliation and the beatings, but more than anything in his life, Zach hated his brother. At almost eighteen, Clifton was a senior at Sir John A. MacDonald and he was a younger brother's worst nightmare. He excelled in academics, hung out with the jocks and the best-looking girls, he was muscular, and just happened to be one of the finest athletes in the school. He was his father's favorite son and after the divorce, Clifton had chosen to live with his dad instead of staying with his mom and Zach. But then dad's drinking never seemed to be a problem for the perfect son.

The drinking was, however, a problem for Zach and his mom, but especially for Zach. He could always count on his dad getting drunk and starting a fight; the problem was, Zach never knew for sure when it would happen. That was the hardest part of living with an alcoholic: you never actually knew what to expect or when to expect it. On the days he did drink, it was pretty much the same. He'd sit in his favorite chair and make Zach mix his drinks. He'd quickly drink his way past the friendly-funny stage to the angry-psycho stage. Once his dad's speeches began, Zach knew it was time to prepare himself for the attacks. Even though the head buzz from too much booze wrecked his dad's sense of balance, this 230 pound angry drunk could still pack a punch. He didn't care where his punches landed or what was in his hand when he swung; most times he didn't even know. His only goal was to inflict pain. As for the speeches, the theme was always roughly the same: Zach was a disappointment and Clifton was a dream come true. Remnants of the last speech still echoed through his memory, like a movie clip stuck on replay. Each time the memory played in his mind, he felt like he was watching images of someone else's life. After a year the images were still fresh, but he'd noticed recently that watching the replay didn't sting quite as much as it once had. In Zach's memory loop, his dad sways and shouts, splashing the dark fluid from his glass all over himself and the carpet. His eyes narrow and his gaze centers somewhere over Zach's head. His mouth fires insults into the air like explosives from a rocket launcher. "You little puke. You've always been a disappointment," he spits as he unbuckles his belt. "Look at yourself, you're nothing like Clifton." This part of the memory clip is the hardest for Zach to watch as, in slow motion, his dad slides his black leather belt through his pant loops. Zach can hear the leather dragging against the cloth and even as he watches from the bleachers of his memory, the smell of the drink nauseates him. "You're a miserable failure. Look at your hair and those crappy clothes. You look like some kind of homeless kid! Your grades are pathetic and you fight with anyone and everyone. I've told you a thousand times, you don't use your fists to solve your problems."

Zach had always been amazed, and even a little amused, that his dad would use this line, but he seemed to be the only one who understood the irony. As the belt slips through the loops, Zach's eyes carefully scan the scene, as he positions himself with room to bob and weave like a boxer in a ring. "You're nothing but a disappointment!" his dad spits, spraying his son carelessly through angry, drunken lips. And then it begins. If all he'd had to endure were beatings, Zach probably could have managed, but it was the constant comparison that enraged him and fueled his hatred. "Look at your brother. He can play ball; he's the best athlete in the school. He's got brains. Clifton's gonna be somebody someday. You're never gonna amount to anything." The memory loop often got stuck on those words, playing them over in bits and bites. "You'll never amount to anything. Not to anything. Nothing . . . You're nothing." And then his dad's lips curl in rage. He sets the drink on the counter and with hatred in his voice, folds his weapon in half and brings it down with a slap on the face of his drink-less hand. "You need me to show you how to be a man - one day you're gonna thank me for this." And with this commitment to his son's painful education, the belt flies through the air, missing Zach's shoulder and slapping him on the right side of his neck and jaw and then curling around to hit him again in the middle of his back. He would feel the flesh of a fist and the bite of the belt and always that vile smell filling his senses. Always that smell. And then, without warning, the screen would fade to black. And that's where the memory loop always stopped and without a moment to catch his breath, it would begin again, filling his senses with unstoppable images and always those words, "You little puke . . . You're nothing."

After his dad had sobered up, he would often come to Zach, not to apologize, but to make his threatening deal. But whether he came or not, Zach knew there was always the threat. "Our play fights are our little secret, son. You ever tell anyone, and I mean anyone, and you'll find out what a real beating feels like!" Zach hated himself for keeping the secret. Maybe his dad was right about him. Maybe he was a coward. He hated himself for being afraid and for not being able to protect himself. He'd never told anyone, but for years fear had immobilized him. When his dad came at him with the belt, Zach would stand frozen to the floor, trembling but unable to move, terrified and unable to breathe. On many occasions he would lose control of his bladder, and as his dad approached, he would feel the warm liquid running down his legs. In the year before the divorce, Zach had figured that standing still wasn't the best strategy and he'd learned that with the slightest turn of his body, he could sidestep a swing. He'd also discovered that the energy of fear could be translated into rage and rage replaced helplessness with power. As he grew in size and began to win fights at school, Zach's confidence grew and his fear no longer paralyzed him as it once had. These days he was feeling something different. Deep down inside he felt a determination, a feeling that he hadn't yet put to words, but that pressed against his will like the slow steady weight of too much water pressing against an unstable dam. It was a powerful, intoxicating feeling, and Zach knew that soon his dam was going to break, and when it did, there would be no fear, and no regret. Someday soon, someone was going to pay.

After all of this, his dad had finally been forced to leave. One night, after a severe beating that left Zach with permanent damage to his right eye, his mom had finally had enough. She'd called the police and within hours the drunk was gone. They'd seen him at the custody hearings, but he hadn't so much as looked at them and he certainly had never acknowledged any wrongdoing. The judge had taken the assault seriously and Zach's dad was told that he was not to be within 500 feet of either Zach or his mother for any reason. Failure to adhere to these rules would result in a prison term. Some recognition of wrongdoing would have been nice, but for Zach and his mom, the space to live their lives in safety was enough. After years of living in fear, Zach and his mom were free. It was a fresh start but the joy was short-lived. Shortly after his dad had left, Zach's mom had crashed into a deep depression and only now was she starting to come to life again.

"Fixing her hair," Zach thought to himself with a smile, "that's got to be a good sign." For weeks his mom could barely get out of bed, but this morning, things felt different. She was up early, she had a new job to go to, and she was even fixing her hair. Zach was feeling like this might be the beginning of a great day. "I got the door; you keep working on that hair. From what I can see you'll need a whole lot more time," Zach teased as he passed the open bathroom door.

"Hey, watch it, smart mouth. Old people have feelings too," his mom replied, throwing a wet towel and just missing his head. It was unusual to have someone banging on the door this early in the morning and annoying to have someone knocking with such persistence.

"Man, what's with the psycho door pounding? It's a beautiful day - chill out!" Zach called out to the door. Getting a little irritated he yelled over his shoulder, "This guy needs to cut back on the caffeine," but his mom didn't hear him over the noise of the blow dryer. Zach removed the safety chain and, as he opened the door, a familiar smell assaulted his senses and smoldered into the room as his eyes fell on the one person he'd hoped he'd never see again. As his glare bore a hole in the face with the crooked smile, Zach felt deep within him dark waters pressing against the wall of his dam and he knew that very soon something was going to crack.

"Hey, you little puke, where's your mother?" said his dad as he pushed passed Zach and stepped into the living room of the apartment, uninvited.

"None of your business, you're not even supposed to be here, so why don't you just get out?" Zach said as he forced the creeping panic away from his face.

"Zachy, why the negative attitude?" his dad said with a smooth voice dripping with sarcasm.

Zach walked toward the cordless phone, snatched up the receiver, and began to dial. "One call to the police and you'll be in jail, that's what the judge said. Or have you forgotten?" Indeed Zach's confidence had grown in his father's absence, but as often happens in the teen years, he had become overconfident, even cocky, thinking that he could control the situation. With lightening speed, his dad was across the tiny living room floor and before Zach knew what was happening, he'd fastened an iron grip around the arm that held the phone.

"Easy does it shooter, I come in peace. I just want to talk to your mom," he said in a friendly tone. Zach's wrist was beginning to burn,

5

but he kept his eyes locked on his enemy.

"How'd you get in here anyway?" he said in an angry tone. "You were supposed to give your keys to the judge."

"I did give my keys to the judge, but then I found this little fellow loose in one of my drawers. It only opens the main door to the building, but I guess I can always knock on the apartment door. You and your mother will always be stupid enough to let me in."

"You jerk!" Zach said as he tried again to yank his wrist free from the man's vice-grip. Zach's dad held the key in front of his son's eyes with his free hand, taunting and provoking the angry teen. His dad laughed, releasing the smell of alcohol into the air in a disgusting spray of spit.

"I guess this means I'll be coming to visit more often. Maybe we can have some of that good ol' family time, just like the old days."

As those words fell out of his mouth Zach's mom turned off the hair dryer and stepped from the bathroom to see her ex-husband holding Zach firmly by the arm. "Let him go! And get out!" she screamed as she moved toward her ex. She wasn't very big, but Zach's mom could be fierce in a fight. Unlike Zach, she'd never been one to stand and take a beating without delivering a few punches of her own. "I said let him go," as she pulled her son away and stepped between them.

"Hey baby, just a friendly visit. What's everybody all hostile about this morning?" he said, his eyes sparkling with enjoyment. Zach's dad stepped back and began to stroll slowly around the room. Reaching inside his coat, he pulled out his pack of smokes and lit up, drawing on the smoke and blowing it out through his nose.

"You know you're not supposed to come within 500 feet, so I suggest you turn around and go through that door. We don't want you here!" Zach's mom said in a strong, confident voice.

"I'm going, baby. I just wanted you to know that Clifton's getting an athletic award tonight. Athlete of the year at MacDonald. I wasn't sure this little puke would tell you about it." He took another long drag on his smoke and seated himself confidently on the arm of the old couch he'd bought at a garage sale.

Her eyes were ablaze with fire. "I don't need you to deliver messages to me and I don't ever want to hear you speak about Zach like that again!" she said. "Now take your cigarette smoke and get out."

"Not a problem, sorry Zachy. I guess I need to work on my manners," he said sarcastically through another cloud of smoke and one of his twisted smirks. "You know, it really is too bad that Zachy isn't getting any awards this year. Perhaps Clifton will let you touch his trophy if you ask him real nice," he said in his own uniquely irritating and mocking tone.

"I could care less about Clifton, or his stupid trophy, or you, so why don't you just get out?" Zach said as he was beginning to find some confidence. He had forgotten how strong his dad was and both he and his mom knew that if this man wanted to do some damage, neither of them would be able to stop him. Zach could feel a tinge of fear growing within him, but he forced himself to translate the feelings into hatred and rage. Instead of backing down, he found himself stepping forward, again overestimating his abilities. "You might be able to grab my arm now, but after you're gone, I'm calling the police and you're going to jail," Zach said. His dad raised his arm and smirked, but instead of lashing out, he simply stared at the small silver object he held between his finger and thumb. He spoke in a low confident voice, "They might lock me up, but they can't keep me forever and I'll always be able to find a key to the door you're hiding behind. And one night you're gonna wake up with me standing over you and it's gonna be payback for all that crap you fed the judge about me during the hearings. Someday soon, I'm gonna show you what a real beating feels like."

"That's enough," Zach's mom said as she stepped between the two warriors preparing to engage in battle. "We get your point, we're not going to call the police, but we need your promise that you're not going to be barging in here whenever you want."

"A promise? Sure baby, I promise. I promise that I won't show up, unless I feel like it. How's that?" Zach's dad laughed and reached for the door knob. "It sure would be nice, Zachy, if you would come and celebrate Clifton's success with us tonight. It may be the only chance you get to see your last name on a trophy," he said through his crooked smile as he opened the door. "I'm glad we've been able to share some family time. I'll drop by again, but next time Zach, you and me are gonna have some *real* father-son time," and this time his dad's voice dropped in volume and his right hand moved to gently tap the buckle on his black leather belt. He blew a long stream of smoke into Zach's face and laughed as he slammed the door shut behind him. Zach and his mom stood in the smoky-silence, helplessly enraged by the presence of this menace and sickened by the stale smell of alcohol, a smell they had both had come to detest.

For a few moments the room was painfully silent. "Celebrate Clifton's award," Zach snapped, "Is he insane?" "He doesn't care about a judge's orders. He doesn't care about any 500 foot rule. He's gonna do what he wants and nobody's going to be able to stop him!"

"Zach that's not true," his mom said. "We just have to work things out with him. There's no sense getting the police involved again if we don't have to." Zach stood staring at the door, his fists clenched by his sides, his knuckles burning white. His jaw was set, his eyes were on fire, and hatred burned in his chest. And in that moment of rage, he made up his mind. It was time. Time to do something. Time to hurt the one who had made a sport of hurting him and if he couldn't do it by beating him physically, he'd do it by hurting the only person his dad had ever seemed to care about. This would be the ultimate insult, the greatest pain he could inflict for his years of suffering. Clifton would never make it to tonight's banquet, and Zach would make sure that MacDonald's athlete of the year would never see his name on that trophy.

~ 2 FAMILY ~

"Good morning Lex, how did you sleep?" asked Rebecca, as if she fully expected the skinny black lab to give her a detailed answer. "And Lady, how's your leg this morning? You still look pretty tired. Just a few more days and you can go home." Although Rebecca spoke in soft tones, the entire room was in a barking-uproar. Rapid-fire yelps from the small breeds threatened to shatter your ear drums, and the deep base barks from the large breeds rattled the kennel doors. "Yes, I can hear you too Mason. You're pretty hard to ignore." She spoke to each patient as she passed the cages, heading for the loudest of the pack. Mason was Rebecca's favorite. A gentle golden retriever, he'd been in the hospital a number of times over the past few months and he and Rebecca had become friends. He was up in years, probably around thirteen, Rebecca thought. He was a little heavier than he needed to be and the silver lines around his eyes gave him the look of a wise elder. Although he was very sick and some of his body functions had slowed, his age had not yet impaired his ability to bark. As soon as Rebecca propped her bike against the wall in the alley behind the veterinary hospital at 6:30 a.m., Mason would begin to call. He'd been with them now for four days, and yesterday she'd tried her best to sneak up on him. Instead of riding up to the hospital's back door, she'd walked her bike up slowly, gently leaning the frame against the wall. Walking quietly toward the back door to let herself in, she was sure she'd beaten him. But before she could insert the key into the lock, Mason had started into a rant of barking, which of course signaled the alert to every other imprisoned canine, sending the room into a deafening frenzy that could not be silenced. "I just can't fool you, Mason! You've got amazing ears for an old grandpa dog," she said over the din. Unlatching the cage door, a searching, dry black-snout pressed toward her, filling itself with her sweet odor, sniffing and snorting and snuffing her in with dog-like passion. "There ya go big guy, how does that feel?" she asked as she rubbed his ears and back and chest. "Let's get you outside so you can stretch your legs, then we'll get you some food and do a little house cleaning." Mason looked up at her with his affectionate, deep brown eyes, his entire body in motion in response to a backend that seemed to have a mind of its own. Rebecca was his friend and everything was perfect when they were together.

On Monday, Wednesday, and Sunday, Rebecca was always the first one at the hospital. It had been this way for almost two years now. Her first visit had been difficult. Rebecca's mom had hit Dexter, their own dog, while backing out of the driveway. They'd brought him straight to the hospital and within a few months of the accident, he was back to his old self. Dr. Kristin Anderson had included Rebecca in every step of the healing process. As a matter of fact, things had gone so well between them that Dr. Anderson had invited Rebecca to volunteer at the hospital and had even encouraged her to consider a career in veterinary medicine. Rebecca fed the animals, took them outside, coaxed them to take some of their medication, and even changed some of the dressings when other vet assistants were there to help. Her mother had suggested on several occasions that Rebecca consider getting a job where she'd actually get paid. She didn't seem to understand that caring was the most meaningful and wonderful thing Rebecca could possibly do. She loved her work at the hospital and when she wasn't there she often found herself thinking about the animals, and counting the minutes until she could return. Although it wasn't part of her normal volunteer schedule, Rebecca would often pop in on her way home from school just to check on the patients, provide a few extra pats and kind words, and spend a few moments talking with the staff and, if she was available, to Dr. Anderson.

"OK everybody, have a good day. I'll see you on Wednesday," Rebecca called out to a room full of barking objections. She laughed as she pulled the door closed, unlocked her bike, and headed for home. It may have been early on a Monday morning, but at least the sun was warm enough to chase the morning chill from the air. She breathed deeply, taking a moment to enjoy the fresh contrast. She loved animals, but sometimes those cages could get pretty stinky. Somehow the outside air always seemed just a little bit sweeter after she'd cleaned the pens. Living ten minutes from the hospital had its advantages, the main one being that a shower was always close by. Having finished her morning routine with the animals, Rebecca was looking forward to cleaning up and getting some breakfast before she'd have to load her backpack and head off for school. She rode up her driveway, leaned her bike against the garage and jogged around to the side door that opened into a small mud room. "Dexter, what have you done?" said Rebecca as she stared into a pair of guilty brown eyes. "Did you eat one of my shoes again?" she asked her chocolate lab as she removed her runners and playfully tugged at the rubber bone he held in his mouth like a trophy. He dropped the offering at her feet and began his homecoming ritual of nuzzling, licking, and general dog dancing wiggles that were enough to make one think that she'd been gone for at least a year when it had only been about an hour.

Passing through the kitchen, Rebecca could hear her mom already on the phone with a client talking about water damage in a basement. After watching her mom for several years, Rebecca knew one thing for sure: she'd never want to sell real estate. It seemed like her mom was always rushed and always dealing with unexpected problems. It was a fast-paced job, but she had a knack for multi-tasking that made her good at what she did. "Hey Dad," Rebecca called out as she made her way through the den and toward the stairs that led to her bedroom.

"Dr. Doolittle I presume," her dad called out in an English accent, sounding like the actors she'd heard on his old Monty Python DVD. Not too long ago he had finally convinced her to sit with him for a full evening to watch *The Holy Grail*. As she watched, she'd gotten the impression that the actors had borrowed twenty dollars and taken a couple of hours to make a movie. It was awful. But her dad had laughed himself silly, constantly pointing at the TV, mimicking the memorized lines with a similar accent, slapping his leg, and wiping the tears from his eyes. Who says there's no generation gap? she'd thought to herself.

"And how was your visit with your little flock of dogs this morning?" he said not looking up from his morning paper and struggling to hold his lame English accent.

"Great dad, but dogs don't usually travel in flocks," she teased, using a voice that teens reserve for parents who say things that aren't very smart.

"Ah yes, yes, my mistake, my mistake. Let me try again. How was your pack of Rufus Canis this fine day?" he asked like a Latin scholar while tossing the rubber bone for Dexter and trying hard not to lose his composure.

"They're fine dad. You know you're not a normal man?" she said as she continued toward the stairs.

"Not normal?" he said, faking a hurt and surprised tone and still working his English accent. "I used to be normal. Then I had a teenager!" he shouted after her, as she took the stairs two at a time.

Heading into her room, she shook her head in amusement and laughed softly to herself. Her dad was such a nut and she loved him with all her heart. With the stories she constantly heard from friends, she knew her relationship with her dad was amazing. For one thing, she got to live in the same house with him. Lots of her friends only got to see their dads on weekends. One of Rebecca's friends had just told her last week how she wanted to have a relationship with her dad like Rebecca had with hers. She'd complained that it was just too difficult to get close when her dad's girlfriend was always trying to build a meaningful relationship with her. Rebecca's dad respected her and treated her like a person, not a little girl, or a problem teen. Sure, they'd had their tense moments, but he always took time to listen and to help her, rather than attempting to solve her problems for her. They had a friendship, but what else could she have with a man who cared deeply for her, loved dogs, had a very odd sense of humour, and was constantly speaking in strange accents and creating new words out of thin air?

Before jumping into the shower, Rebecca selected her clothes for the day and laid them out neatly on her bed. As she was heading into the bathroom, she heard the email tone on her computer, indicating that someone had just sent her a message. She quickly checked her inbox and found a note from Amy.

"Hey girl, are we still meeting for lunch in the cafeteria? There's something I really need to talk with you about." Amy knew Rebecca's schedule pretty well and knew her routine included the hospital, a shower, and breakfast. She was pretty sure she could catch her with an email before Rebecca headed off for school.

Rebecca quickly replied, "Not a problem. I hope everything's OK. I'll see you at 12."

Twenty-minutes later, Rebecca felt refreshed and eager to enjoy the sunshine that awaited her. As she made her way into the kitchen in search of breakfast, Dad and Dexter greeted her with smiles. It was rare to share breakfast with her dad, but now that his university teaching was over for another semester, they had more opportunity to spend time together. Rebecca's mom had slipped into her office looking for a pen and, by the time she joined them in the kitchen, she was already running through her mental checklist of things that needed be done.

"Becky honey, did you remember to put that load in the wash like I asked?"

"Ya Mom, I did. And did you remember my name's Rebecca? Not Becky,"

Rebecca said kindly as she kissed her mom on the forehead. Rebecca and her mom had a great relationship, even though they were completely different. During the past year, they'd talked frequently about Rebecca's future, about her becoming a woman, and about the kinds of things moms and daughters talk about when dads aren't around. Rebecca had decided that her little girl 'Becky' days were behind her and, although it had been a difficult series of conversations, her mom had agreed. They had agreed that Becky would cease to exist and that strong, confident Rebecca would take her place. But, as can often happen, mom was having a hard time letting go of her little Becky.

"What? Becky? Oh yes, I've done it again haven't I?" her mother said, in a voice that told Rebecca that the name change was getting on her nerves. "Promise me that you won't go play at that silly animal hospital after school. You know I have to be at MacDonald early to help with the awards ceremony." She continued talking to herself absent-mindedly, as some mothers are in the habit of doing, as she buttered a muffin. "I can't remember exactly what I'm doing at the banquet. I'm sure someone will tell me what to do as soon as I get there. Oh and Becky honey, make sure that Baxter gets what he needs before you come over to MacDonald."

"'Becky' and 'Baxter' Mom? Are you feeling alright? My name's Rebecca and our dog is Dexter."

Ignoring her daughter's protests, Rebecca's mom stopped to kiss her smirking husband on the top of his head. "Goodbye dear," she said.

"You know, it really would be good if you could get their names right," Rebecca's dad said in a voice quivering on the edge of laughter.

She returned his smirk, "Yes dear, I'll put that on my list of things to do." Then she touched Rebecca on the cheek and looked into her eyes, "We're so proud of you Rebecca. It's going to be another wonderful night of celebration. Now let me see: keys, my glasses, I've got my cell. My briefcase? Where has my briefcase gone to?"

"It's in the mud room Mom, I saw it when I came in," Rebecca said as she watched her mom with some amusement.

"OK then, I think I've got everything. I love you all, have a great day. I'll see you around 4:30, Becky." And with that she closed the door and was gone. Rebecca sighed deeply. She and her dad sat for a few moments looking at each other and then without warning both burst into laughter, shaking their heads, not quite believing what they'd just seen and heard. Rebecca took her dishes to the sink, gave her dad a pat on the back, rubbed Dexter's nose and headed for the door.

"Will you be at MacDonald tonight Dad?" she asked in a voice that told him she was teasing.

Stoking up his English accent, he began playfully imitating her mom, "I do believe that someone from our own household is receiving an award tonight. Let me see now, who could that be? I seem to have forgotten. Perhaps someone will tell me when I get there." They both laughed again.

"This family is seriously strange," she said smiling, as she put on her shoes. "I'll see you tonight." And with that, she was out the door and on her way. Of course, there was no way that Rebecca could have known that she would never make it to the awards banquet, that she would never walk across the stage to receive her academic honor. There was also no way she could have known that by midnight, her ability to care for her friends would be put to the test as she faced the most pain-filled day of her young life.

~ 3 Deep Listening ~

As she turned onto James Street heading toward MacDonald, Rebecca's nose caught the smell of lilac, moments before her eyes feasted on the midsized tree full of beautiful purple flowers. The rich fragrance filled her senses and made her want to stop and have a picnic with her closest friends, right under the flowering bouquet. The sun was warm and the crispness had all but dissolved. With her mind working hard to devise a plan to get through the back door without Mason hearing her, she almost missed the lone figure sitting on the stairs of the apartment complex across the road. The figure sat motion-less, a black hood from a sweater pulled over his head. It could have been a monk deep in thought, but it was Zach. "Hey Zach, are you coming?" she called as she often did when she bumped into him on the way to school. But strangely, this time, there was no response. Rebecca knew he often walked around listening to music through small black plugs that fit right into his ears. If he had those in this morning, there'd be no way he'd hear her. She got off her bike and crossed the street to see if she could get his attention. She was almost standing on his toes before he looked up to see her sun-washed smile. As their eyes met, Rebecca felt awkward; it seemed like Zach wasn't very happy to see her.

Great. A happy person. Just what I need right now, Zach thought to himself as he removed the earplugs and nodded a silent greeting. It had been about half an hour since his dad had left, plenty of time for Zach to stow his anger until he might need it again. Sitting on the steps and savouring the fresh air was helping him to clear his head and prepare to face the world.

"Well, are you just gonna sit there all day looking grumpy or what?" Rebecca demanded. "It's almost summer! The sun is shining. Life is good Zach. Let's get going." But Zach didn't move and he didn't speak, he just looked down at his feet and sat very still. Immediately Rebecca sensed that something was wrong. Putting her bike on its stand, she sat down slowly beside Zach. "What is it Zach? What's going on? Has something happened? Is your mom alright?"

Zach rose to his feet and, forcing a smile, began to walk. As Rebecca joined him he simply replied, "I just didn't sleep well last night, that's all." As soon as the words came out of his mouth, Zach felt the bitter aftertaste of keeping a secret he no longer wanted to guard. He felt the sickness churn in his stomach as he thought of all the times he'd been asked, "Zach, is something wrong?" And he thought of all the times he'd lied, not knowing how to say, "Well actually yes, there is something wrong. My dad's a drunk and I'm terrified of him because he beats me." That explanation might have worked when Zach was eight years old, but now it just sounded lame and pathetic. It was so much easier to keep the secret than to explain the truth. But the secret was killing him. If he ever wanted to be free, truly free, Zach knew he'd have to tell someone how he really felt. As they walked slowly together, he glanced over at Rebecca from under his hood. They'd been friends for years and had passed through a time when they'd even talked about dating. But as he compared his life with hers, his future with hers, his brains with hers, his friends with hers, it just didn't look like a match made in heaven. Zach took a deep breath and made a decision. Feeling uncertain and standing on unstable legs, he knew that he would need to summon all of his courage. Once he took this step, there would be no turning back. This wasn't talking to a judge to get his dad kicked out of the house; this was something different. Zach was going to talk about himself. He was going to ask for help, not to hurt his enemy, but to find some peace. Stopping on the sidewalk, Zach turned slowly and reaching up, he pulled his hood down and rested it on his shoulders. Rebecca could see that he'd been crying, but not wanting him to feel embarrassed, she chose not to ask. The silence between them wasn't awkward. Somehow it seemed natural, even comfortable for them to stand together in the morning sun, listening to the mix of city sounds and the odd bird song. Rebecca made space for him. Choosing not to fill the silence with her own words, she simply waited.

Finally, Zach was ready. "Rebecca, can I tell you something?" Feeling the weight in his voice and looking into his sad, serious face, she knew that the conversation they were about to have couldn't happen on the street or at MacDonald.

"Sure Zach," she said. "Do you wanna grab a drink and talk for a bit?" she asked. "Yeah, I think I'd like that. But what about class? I don't want to get you in trouble for skipping."

"Zach, this sounds important. I don't think missing one math class is going to wreck my grade point average."

He chuckled self-consciously and looked at his feet for a moment, "Yeah, missing one class isn't gonna change my grades much either. Thanks Rebecca," he said as they started to walk. "But I have to warn you, I've got some pretty messed up stuff to talk about."

"Well, it can't be any worse than the story I heard from Mason this morning," she said with a chuckle.

"Mason? Who's Mason?" Zach asked.

Rebecca laughed again, "Just this dreamy red-headed guy I've been spending some time with. Maybe after you've told me your messed up stuff, I can tell you about my love life."

Zach snickered a little. "Love life? That sounds a whole lot more interesting than what I've got to say, maybe you should go first."

Rebecca was smiling a mischievous grin enjoying the game she was playing with Zach. "Maybe after our chat I can introduce you to Mason. I bet you'll feel better just running your fingers through his long red hair. It always helps me."

"Uh, yeah, whatever," Zach said, giving her a suspicious glance. Her laugh told him she was teasing, and looking at her he could see the mischief in her eyes. Zach smiled back, shaking his head. Maybe this wouldn't be such a bad day after all.

As they drank their coffee, Rebecca listened deeply and with her caring as Zach found the courage to tell his story and to speak honestly about some of his fears. It was an amazing contrast for him, given the way his day had begun. It seemed that no one had ever listened to him with such kindness and so little interest in judgment. He felt safe. As Zach described his dad's eyes, and the smell in the room, Rebecca could picture his images in her mind. At first she was fine but, as the story got darker, she began to feel afraid, to feel his terror deep within her, and then his outrage.

How could a father do these things! she thought to herself. But then a stab of guilt hit her hard. I've known Zach for years. Why didn't I know he was in trouble? How could I have missed the bruises? How could I have let this happen? she thought to herself. Zach told her of the video loop that tormented him constantly and the words that had broken his heart. Tears streamed down her friend's face as he choked on the words in anger, "You little puke, you're nothing." And Rebecca found that tears were slipping from her own eyes and horror sat on her shoulders like a heavy weight, pressing her down into her seat, forcing her to sit still, helplessly watching her friend. All these years of pain and she hadn't known. She'd done nothing to help him. The guilt kept nagging at her, trying to steal her attention away from the story.

Zach hadn't planned on describing the beatings in detail, but somehow his story was rushing out, taking on a life of its own, needing to be emptied from his heart like dumping putrid, bug-infested water from an old rain barrel. And right when she thought she'd heard the worst of it, he began to describe the attacks. Slowly, he described the sound of his dad's belt sliding through the loops and the sound of leather on denim. He closed his eyes and in vivid detail described his dad's drink sloshing onto the floor, and the weapon, and the flesh pounding into him. Zach told her how he'd cried, begging his dad to stop, and how his father had responded, "One day you'll thank me for teaching you how to be a man."

Rebecca felt sick to her stomach. How to be a man! she thought to herself. This guy doesn't know the first thing about being a father or a man. Horrified and filled with rage at the injustice and violation, she stared at her cold coffee, ashamed that in that moment she couldn't think of a single thing to say. Having nothing to relieve his suffering, Rebecca felt guilt edging its way slowly up her throat and helplessness gripped her. She'd known things had been rough for him during the divorce and she'd thought she understood, but obviously she didn't have a clue what his life had really been like. Now she was working hard to keep her full attention on Zach. She was finding it increasingly difficult to listen and manage her own internal world. What can I say to help him? How can I make this pain stop? What kind of monster would beat his little boy? Her questions were overwhelming her like hundreds of emails arriving in an inbox at the same time and she felt like she was about to crash.

Then, as suddenly as it had begun, Zach came to the end of his story and breathed a sigh of relief. As his story had toppled out, he'd decided not to speak about his decision to keep Clifton from getting the award. That was something he was still chewing on. Besides, Clifton and Rebecca were friends too, and there was no way she was going to stand by and watch them hurt each other. Talking about his messed up life was enough for now. He'd keep his plans to himself and she'd find out when everyone else did. Rebecca looked up at the clock over the pop machine; it had been two hours since she'd first seen him sitting on the apartment steps. "I guess I really needed to talk," he said wiping his eyes on the sleeve of his sweater. "Sorry about that. That's a lot to take in all at once."

"No Zach, this was important, don't apologize. I'm fine, I'm just glad you were able to get that stuff out." Rebecca could hear her voice speaking kindly to Zach, but somehow it sounded hollow and far away. She was numb, tingling like her limbs had all gone to sleep. And she felt a deep sadness in her bones. Zach had a smile on his face that told her that a thousand pounds had been lifted from his chest; secrets are always heavy. Rebecca smiled, but her head was full of fog. She gave herself a quick shake and managed a few moments of self-talk as they walked. OK girl, get a grip. You've missed the whole morning of classes. You need to get with Amy and you need to do some damage control with a few teachers. Rebecca checked her schedule in her mind as she felt the fresh air clearing her head. Talking with Zach may have been a rough way to start the day, but seeing the weight lifted off his shoulders made it all worth while. Rebecca was feeling a little worn out, but she'd felt this way before after helping a friend. It wasn't a big deal, besides, she had other things to think about.

~ 4 Unacceptable Gifts ~

"**I** hate you! I'm not going! I'll run away and you'll never find me. I'll go to Toronto and live on the streets!" As she sat in her history class watching the hands of the clock turn in slow motion, Amy let the words play over in her head. It seemed like just yesterday she'd stood on the balcony of her apartment in London, Ontario, screaming those words at her mom and her mom's boyfriend. But that was four years ago. She smiled to herself as she thought about how mouthy she'd been, even at thirteen. "As brave as she was stupid," that's what her mom had said. As she played the memory over in her mind instead of doing the worksheet on her desk, she remembered that it had been October when she'd first heard the news. She'd just started grade eight and the work was turning out to be much harder than she'd anticipated. For one thing, it seemed like she always had homework. Most nights her mom would head out with friends, leaving Amy to clean up the supper mess and take care of her younger brother, David. She also had the challenge of getting him to turn off his PlayStation, so he would go to bed on time. Being only two years younger, he wasn't crazy about being told what to do by his big sister, especially when it had to do with turning off his game, or going to bed. Of course, taking care of the house, and David, meant her homework was often left undone.

Her mom had been looking for work for months while they tried to get by on her unemployment checks. When she got the job offer from a cousin who owned a bakery in Winnipeg, she jumped at the opportunity, but of course it meant they'd have to move. Amy had been furious. She hated the idea of leaving her home and her friends and her school. She and her friends had been talking for months about their new school and how they'd take it by storm, like fashion-models crashing a party. With their new freedom, they'd stay out later, go to dances together, check out guys together, and try out for soccer. It would be the best years of their young lives. But moving meant that Amy would miss it all. And leaving in January meant that she'd have to try to fit into a new school, half way through the year. By the time parents left their teen years, most of them had forgotten just how difficult this kind of transition could be.

Her mother had simply said, "Don't worry, you'll make new friends." But for a thirteen year-old girl, it was a living nightmare. As it turned out, Amy failed that year and had to repeat grade eight. That made her popular for all the wrong reasons. Not only was she an outsider from Ontario, but she was a stupid outsider; a failure. Her first year at MacDonald hadn't been much better. It wasn't until the summer just before her junior year that things began to improve. She and Rebecca had both signed up in the spring to play soccer for the same league and, by the end of the season, they were friends for life. Rebecca's friendship had helped Amy face the despair of another year in a school full of strangers, another year alone. She truly was a best friend.

Amy's mind drifted back to her history room as the buzzer signaled the end of class and the beginning of lunch. Normally this was her favorite time of day. The two girls would often find a corner and talk the hour away as they shared their lunches, their lives, and their love for animals. Rebecca would often describe her experiences in the hospital, keeping Amy up to date on the patients and their progress. But today would be different. In grade ten and almost seventeen, Amy felt like she was re-living the nightmare of her thirteenth year, something she'd promised herself she'd never, ever go through again. And she fully intended to keep that promise, even if it meant taking her own life.

While Amy sat daydreaming in her history class, Rebecca was up to her ears in damage control. Her first conversation with her math teacher had gone well. Mr. Donaldson and Rebecca knew each other from the fundraising project that student council had organized early in the semester. During their work together, he'd made a point on several occasions of telling her how much he'd appreciated her maturity and brilliance, and he'd made a habit of encouraging her to consider a career in the sciences. "You know Rebecca," he'd say in a booming voice, "there's plenty of room for brilliant young women like yourself in the sciences. Plenty of room." In his years at MacDonald, very few students had been able to demonstrate the kind of grasp she had for mathematics and it was more than a pleasure for him to see one student actually get it. And not only get it, but he knew that she could easily teach his material if given the chance. His respect for her and the fact that she'd never missed a single one of his classes made him generous and understanding when she explained what had happened that morning. He told her that she'd done a good thing, but to consider moving her counseling hours so that they didn't conflict with her classes. She agreed that she wouldn't let it happen again and thanked him for his understanding.

Rebecca had chosen the easier teacher first, leaving her English teacher, Ms. Crandle, for the second conversation. "And where have you been, miss academic scholar?" Ms. Crandle remarked in a tone that said, "Being smart does not exempt you from attending my class."

"Well that's what I'm here to speak with you about, do you have a moment?"

"I suppose I can give you a few moments, although I am on my way to lunch. Let's hear it," barked Ms. Crandle, fully expecting to hear yet another 'my dog ate my homework,' story.

"Well, I missed class this morning and . . ."

"Brilliant, you must have taken public speaking. Very well organized. Is there anything else you'd like to tell me before I run off for lunch?"

Rebecca straightened up and decided to change her posture from humility to aggressor, but just as she opened her mouth to speak, she drew a complete blank. "I'm sorry Ms. Crandle, I can't seem to remember what I was going to say. I missed class this morning and . . ." Rebecca stammered, unsure of herself and feeling a little wobbly in the legs. Images of a young Zach crying in front of a huge man kept interfering, filling up her memory space, and de-railing her train of thought. Ms. Crandle had no idea what was going on, and Rebecca didn't know how to tell her.

"Rebecca, you must have come to remind me that you missed class so that I would be sure to mark you absent? Thank you. Now perhaps you could show me your doctor's note?"

"Ahh, I'm sorry, I don't have a note. I was talking to a friend and . . ."

"Talking to a friend does not qualify as a valid reason for missing one of my classes, now does it Rebecca? I'm afraid you'll need to have this conversation with Mr. Edwards. I'll check in with his office after lunch, to make sure you've dropped in for a visit. Why don't you get back to me once you've spoken with him? I believe his office has a term for talking to friends instead of attending class: I think they call it *skipping*! Be sure to pick up the assigned readings for tomorrow. You'll find the sheet on the corner of my desk. Now, if you'll excuse me, I do have a lovely tomato sandwich waiting for me." And with that she started down the hall, her heels clicking out disapproval on the linoleum like a hammer pounding nails into the lid of an old wooden coffin.

And Rebecca stood and watched her go, feeling tired and a little out of place and whispering softly to herself, "I hate Mondays."

Mr. Edwards was the vice-principal of MacDonald and involving his office was going to make things complicated. Rebecca had never had to deal with the vice-principal directly, but she knew that the discipline for skipping ranged from after-school detentions to suspension. In either case, with her mom being on the Parent Advisory Committee, she was sure her parents would find out, and no doubt her mother would have a fit. But it was time for lunch and, seeing as Mr. Edwards would be out of his office until one o'clock, she might as well keep her meeting with Amy. Her meeting with Amy! What time was it? She checked her watch, "Just great!" she said to an empty classroom, disappointed in herself for not remembering her meeting. Ten after twelve? Not good! I hope she's still there.

As her mind switched to thoughts of Amy, Rebecca felt a tinge of guilt. She hadn't thought about her friend all morning. Listening to Zach's story and untangling her mess for skipping had all but consumed her, and she still felt out of breath and scatter-brained. Reading Amy's email seemed like yesterday. What was it she'd written? Rebecca tried to remember. Was it something she wanted to tell me, or did she tell me something that she wanted me to remember? She was drawing another blank, just as she'd done in Ms. Crandle's room. "I just can't seem to keep things straight today. I gotta get my brains in gear," she mumbled to herself. And she set off at a quick pace for the cafeteria.

~

"You gonna eat those fries?" said a guy sitting in the chair next to Amy. She gave him a well rehearsed drop-dead look and, without saying a word, let him know that she'd rather give herself a root-canal than share the fries with him.

"Well, they're just sitting there getting cold; don't get all witchy on me." Grunting and looking annoyed, he grabbed his tray and his backpack and motioned with his head to indicate to his friend that it was time to move to another table. Amy was fine sitting alone with her dark thoughts. She looked again at her watch and scanned the cafeteria with her red, swollen eyes. I wonder what's up with Rebecca? she thought to herself. It's not like her to forget a lunch date. Scanning the cafeteria again, Amy's eyes caught sight of Rebecca on the far side near the main doors. She was busy searching the hundreds of faces, chair by chair, table by table, when she saw Amy stand, over near the windows, giving a slight wave.

"Finally," they both said under their breath at the same time. "Hey Amy, sorry I'm late. It's been a crazy morning."

"Not a problem. I was starting to wonder if you'd forgotten," Amy said with a note of sadness in her voice.

Rebecca was gifted in her ability to sense even the slightest hint of emotion in a person's voice and her empathy provided the sensitivity to move toward pain and not away from it. She didn't understand people who shrugged off suffering like they might brush dandruff off a shirt. To so many of her friends, the pain of other's was sad, but it was simply reality, something to endure, to tolerate, but nothing to get upset about. But to Rebecca, when her friends were in pain, it was always a big deal. Every living, breathing being, whether animal or human, had a right to receive care and attention in its hour of need. "What's up Amy? You sound a little sad. If it's because I'm late, I am sorry but . . ."

"No Rebecca, it's not you, it's just . . ." Amy paused and looked out the window. Right at that moment, it dawned on her that this was going to be hard for Rebecca too. Being focused on her own loss, Amy hadn't even considered how Rebecca might feel. The two looked at each other for a moment, sharing in an unspoken agony. Rebecca stared with searching compassion as she took in the sight of her friend's red swollen eyes. Her heart began to pound. She could feel the sadness seeping from her friend's face; something awful had happened, but what? Rebecca knew better than to rush, simply to get the information she needed to feel better. Instead, she waited. Sitting quietly. Being present. Giving Amy all the time she needed. Finally, Amy took a deep breath and let it out. "Rebecca, I'm moving to Calgary." There was just no easy way to say it and the words hit Rebecca in the chest, knocking the wind from her and leaving her speechless. "Mom's got a chance to open her own bakery and she says the opportunity is just too good to pass up. We're leaving in three weeks." Tears began to stream down Amy's face and Rebecca reached across the table. Without saying a word, she took Amy's hands in hers, letting her own tears fall without reaching up to wipe them away. She didn't care if everyone in the cafeteria saw them hand-in-hand weeping; she just wanted to hold Amy and to somehow take away her pain.

"Amy, I'm so sorry."

After a few moments of silence, Amy reached into her backpack and pulled out a small yellow box. Rebecca recognized it instantly. "I want you to have this," Amy said, as she opened the lid and delicately lifted the slender gold chain from its white cotton bed.

"Amy, that was your grandma's. I can't take that! It's your most precious memory of her. No, I . . ."

But Amy was already pressing the chain into Rebecca's hand. "It's important to me Rebecca. I want you to have this to remember me, after I'm gone."

"Amy, Calgary's not that far. We can spend our summers together and we've still got email." As soon as she'd spoken, Rebecca felt the words fall pathetically from her mouth, to slink shamefully to the floor. And she realized again, as she'd discovered a hundred times before, that sometimes there simply are no words strong enough to lift the weight of sorrow off the shoulders of a friend

"I also want you to have my stereo and my CD's," Amy said, this time not looking into Rebecca's eyes. Amy's face had changed, the sadness replaced with something else. Rebecca watched her closely, puzzled by this odd series of gifts. What's that look in her eye? she thought to herself. And right on the heels of the question came the answer. It was determination. Amy had decided to do something, but what?

"Amy?" Rebecca asked her gently and quietly. But Amy didn't look up. "Amy there's something else. What aren't you telling me?"

Amy knew that lying to Rebecca was almost impossible. She had a way of looking deeply into a person's eyes, and usually within a matter of moments the truth would simply spill out.

"Rebecca, I don't want to hurt you," Amy said trying to avoid those penetrating eyes.

"But it's not your fault, Amy. We're both hurting right now, but we can get through this. It's not your fault."

"You don't understand, Rebecca. I'm not going to Calgary. I can't change schools again. I can't start over. I can't live without you." Rebecca paused for a moment, rapidly processing what she'd just heard. Amy had just entrusted Rebecca with her most treasured possession and now she was telling her that she wasn't moving to Calgary. But hadn't she just said that she wanted Rebecca to remember her, after she was gone?

"Amy, what are you going to do?" Rebecca said firmly.

"I think you know, Rebecca. I don't have any other choice. I can't do this again!" And with that, Amy stood and started walking quickly for the main entrance, her hand squeezed tightly over her mouth, stifling her sobs. Rebecca gathered her things and, checking her watch, quickly followed Amy out to the patch of grass behind the school. It was five minutes to one. Her mind raced as she chased after Amy.

Rebecca spoke out loud, "I wonder what Mr. Edwards will do when he finds out I skipped the morning, the afternoon, and my meeting with him, just to talk to friends?" But for Rebecca, there simply was no choice to make. This was her best friend and it sounded like it might be a matter of life and death.

Amy threw her things on the grass and sat down, pulling her knees up to her chest and wrapping her arms tightly around her legs. She planted her face on the top of her knees and cried quietly for a few moments before looking up. Rebecca had heard enough to suspect what Amy was planning. Last summer, she'd taken a course with her dad that had taught them how to talk with someone in this frame of mind.[1] Rebecca had never in her wildest dreams considered that she

---

[1] Although Rebecca can't remember exactly how to use the model, the Applied Suicide Intervention Skills Training (ASIST) is an excellent resource for helping people work through suicidal thoughts. See the reference list in the back of the book for details.

might use the information she'd learned with her best friend. She hoped she could remember the steps. Before opening her mouth, she pictured the illustration from their workbook and tried to envision the words: explore, ask, listen, review, contract, follow-up. She hadn't actually used it with anyone yet, but this seemed like as good a time as any to give it a shot, especially if it might help keep her friend alive.

"Amy," Rebecca said softly stroking her friend's hair, "Amy, are you trying to tell me that you're thinking about killing yourself?" The impact of those words hit Amy with such force that the flood gates of tears opened wide and the sniffles turned into deep rivers of sobbing grief. Rebecca offered her some Kleenex from her backpack and then leaned into her, holding her close, as they both wept.

"Rebecca, I just don't see any other way out of this. My mom says I have to go. But it's so hard starting over. Killing myself is the only way out."

"So you feel trapped and killing yourself is the only answer."

"Yes, I feel trapped," Amy said quietly.

"Amy this must be so hard for you, to feel like you have to go through this alone," Rebecca said.

"I do feel alone. I mean, no offence, but this is something I have to face by myself and no one can help me."

"I guess you're right Amy," Rebecca said, "this is something you will have to decide for yourself. But you're wrong that you have to go through this alone." Amy lifted her head and met Rebecca's firm and steady eyes, "I'm here with you Amy, and I'm going to help you through this."

Amy nodded, "Thanks for caring Rebecca, but there's nothing you can do." But Rebecca wasn't finished yet. The next part of the model was to ask about the plan, to discover just how lethal or committed this person was to following through.

"Amy, if you went ahead with your plan to kill yourself, how would you do it?" Amy was a little startled by the question. It seemed a little dark for Rebecca to want to know the gory details of a suicide plan.

"I've got some pills for depression that the doctor gave me. I thought if I took them all, that maybe I'd never wake up."

"When were you going to do it?" Rebecca asked, feeling a little bit uncomfortable with the question.

"This Friday, after the dance. I thought that we could have a blast one more time. It's a perfect last memory. I was thinking I'd go home and lock my door and take all my pills. And that would be it."

"Amy, do you have those pills with you now?" Rebecca asked.

"Yes, why?" Rebecca couldn't remember exactly what she was supposed to do next. All she could think about was getting those pills as far away from Amy as she could. "Amy I want you to give me your pills." But Amy's face hardened as she quickly moved away from Rebecca.

"You're going to try to stop me. That's why you're asking me all these questions," Amy said, as she pulled herself out of Rebecca's arms. The tears had stopped and now her puffy eyes were flashing with anger and her jaw was set like a pit-bull locked on a pant leg.

"Of course I'm going to try to stop you, you're my best friend!" Rebecca didn't like the hostile turn the conversation had just taken and she watched helplessly, as Amy scrambled to her feet, picking up her backpack. "Amy, we need to get you some help. We need to talk to someone, together."

"Rebecca, if you're really my friend you won't say a word. If you tell anyone, I mean it, I'll kill myself and it will be your fault!" As soon as she'd said the words, Amy felt sick to her stomach, but it was too late. She needed to die and she couldn't have anyone messing with her plans, not even her most precious friend.

"Amy you know I can't keep a secret like this, you need help." But Amy wasn't listening, she was too busy feeling angry and betrayed, by her former best friend.

"I meant what I said Rebecca, don't say a word to anyone or I mean it, I'll go through with it, just like I said." And with that, she turned and headed out into the parking lot, leaving Rebecca standing helplessly stunned and hopelessly trapped.

~ 5 OUT OF CONTROL ~

It was turning out to be a strange day for Zach. For years now he'd felt like something lived inside his chest, a hungry beast feeding on hatred and rage and growing larger and stronger inside of him. As the beast grew, it needed more room and more hatred and rage to feed on in order to stay strong. Zach had been winning fights and he'd gained a reputation at MacDonald. He was one of the tough guys and even the jocks didn't want to cross him. Although his dad called him little, Zach had grown over the summer and he'd put on enough muscle that now he was intimidating just to look at. But something was wrong and he couldn't quite put his finger on it. He wasn't certain yet, but something inside him had changed during his talk with Rebecca. It was like the balloon in his chest that had been getting bigger and bigger as it filled with rage and hatred over the years, had somehow gotten a tiny hole in it. For the first time in his life, he could sense that his hatred was loosing its grip. It wasn't a comfortable feeling, since hatred had become the center-piece of his personality, the fuel for his merciless fighting techniques, and the guts of who he was. He couldn't remember a time when hatred hadn't consumed him.

But something was changing. As he sat in class listening to the history teacher talking about armed conflicts around the world and the power of peaceful resistance movements, Zach had to laugh to himself. What could peaceful resistance accomplish against skilled fighters? It was a completely foreign idea to him, but immediately, thoughts of Clifton rolled through his mind and a crazy idea landed without invitation or warning. What if Zach actually chose peace instead of violence? What if he chose to become something completely unlike

29

his dad? It's what he'd always wanted, but he'd discovered early on in life just how effective violence could be. He hated what his dad had done to him, but he had to admit that violence was an effective form of communication. Doodling on his notepad absent-mindedly, he wrote his current philosophical inspiration across the top of the page, "Peace is the long way around, but violence is the short-cut that gets results!" He sat with the idea for a moment, trying to think of the results he'd gotten using his fists, but the only results he could think of were the bad ones. It was true that he was feared by many, but at what price? As he walked the halls, he was constantly looking over his shoulder, waiting for someone he'd beaten to come back for a second round. He never knew when some new kid with something to prove would come at him without warning. Being a great fighter meant you constantly had a title to defend, not exactly the kind of results he was hoping for. And then there were the weapons. Winnipeg schools didn't have a lot of guns, but school shootings were always on the news, and there was always a chance that someone would notch things up a bit and decide to by-pass the fists and take a more permanent approach. Zach had often had nightmares of guys he'd beaten, running into a class with a gun screaming his name and shooting randomly, hitting people all over the room and eventually, killing him. It's not something he liked to talk about, but he'd had that nightmare more than once.

His train of thought de-railed, when Zach noticed Mr. Hiebert standing beside his desk staring at him. Actually, he noticed that the entire class was staring at him. "What?" Zach said looking around, trying desperately to retain some level of cool.

"It's good to have you back with us, Zach. Did you enjoy your time away?" Mr. Hiebert asked with a smile and a friendly chuckle. "I don't mean to embarrass you, but I am interested in your response to my question. It's no secret at MacDonald that you are known for choosing violence over peaceful resolution. What do you think then?" But since Zach had been working the idea of peace over in his mind, he didn't have a clue what the teacher was asking him.

"I'm not sure what you mean?" he said sheepishly, as the room filled with mocking giggles.

"I've just told the class why I favor a peaceful response over violence, but seeing as I value other opinions, I am asking you to tell the class why you favor a violent response over peaceful resolution?"

The question was strange, kind of like asking another kid in the class why they chose to breathe, or why they chose to walk upright. Zach had never had it put to him quite like this and it caught him off guard.

After a moment of thought, he responded, "It gets results."

"It gets results," Mr. Hiebert said slowly and thoughtfully as he typed the answer into his laptop so he could project it onto the screen for all to see. "Well said, Zach, and I gratefully accept the challenge," said the teacher with a smile.

"What do you mean?" Zach asked, feeling as though he'd missed something again.

"Zach, you are going to convince the class that peace has created better results for people and for our planet, than violence could ever hope to accomplish. You've just volunteered for a class project and guess who your partner will be?" Mr. Hiebert gave his stunned student a little wave over the edge of the laptop screen to indicate that they'd be working together on the project. The class broke into laughter as the buzzer sounded and Zach's friends mockingly congratulated him with pats on the back as they headed for the door. Zach sat with his head hung in despair, not able to believe what had just happened to him.

Finally, after everyone had left the room, Zach said, "Ah, sir, you're not serious, are you?"

"I am serious Zach, and it will be worth thirty percent of your final grade. Now, before we begin our research, I'd like you to engage in a little field experiment."

"A what?" Zach said, as he stood and threw his backpack over his shoulder.

"An experiment. Sometime before class on Wednesday, I'd like you to insert a peaceful response into a situation where you would normally respond with violence. And I'd like you to write down what happened, how you wanted to respond, and the way your peaceful response changed the results of the situation." Zach was shocked, but a little bit intrigued as well. He was eager to prove that violence would produce better results and that peace was simply another way of admitting weakness and defeat.

"Yeah, OK, I'll do your experiment. But if I prove that violence gets better results, you pick someone else to work with on the class assignment," Zach said with confidence.

"It's a deal," said Mr. Hiebert, stretching out his hand to shake Zach's. "I'll look forward to seeing your results." Of course, Zach had no idea that he wouldn't have to wait until Wednesday to find a violent situation. Clifton was standing in the parking lot waiting for his little brother, and he wasn't in the mood for a peaceful chat.

~

Rebecca almost jumped out of her skin when the final bell rang. She'd been having difficulty concentrating all day, her mind wandering between Zach and Amy. Her thoughts circled in her mind like a search plane with images of Zach's dad, Amy's gold chain, the belt, saying goodbye to Amy at the airport as she flew off to Calgary, a bottle of alcohol, a crying little boy, and Amy's words in the parking lot, "You'd better not tell anyone, or I mean it, I'll kill myself!" Around and around the plane circled, never landing, never slowing down, the thoughts flying in and out like they had a will of their own. She'd jumped when the buzzer rang, startled back into the present, and so glad to have this day over. Zach's story had terrified her, Amy's pain had crippled her, talking to her teachers about skipping had humiliated her, and her conversation with Mr. Edwards had just about killed her. Thankfully, he hadn't suspended her, but he had been clearly disappointed and recommended that she speak to her parents and perhaps to a counselor. Although he'd understood her desire to help her friends, he'd also made it clear that the primary purpose of her being at MacDonald was to get an education, not to run a free counseling service for her friends. There were trained professionals who could provide those services and he strongly encouraged her to pay more attention to her own life and responsibilities, and less attention to those in crisis. Rebecca had been respectful and listened carefully, up until she heard those words. She just couldn't understand how people could be so callous. It seemed like even teachers and high school administrators didn't care about hurting people as much as she did. Sometimes it felt like she was the only one who truly cared enough to do something for people in need.

"At least Monday's over," she said to herself, as she headed out the back door of the school toward her bike. Pulling her ride away from the stand, she noticed Zach walking ahead of her toward the main road that would take him to his apartment complex. He'd been walking around the outside of the school in search of Clifton and was about to give up and head for home. Zach had been determined this morning to take his anger out on the trophy winner, but his mood had changed since then. He wasn't sure now what he'd do if he actually ran into him. Rebecca could see that Zach's attention was glued on a crowd that seemed to be making its way quickly toward him. It was something he'd witnessed a hundred times or more. This was a mob, thirsty for blood. There was going to be a fight and it looked like he was the guest of honour. Zach put his pack down and waited as the mob split down the middle, allowing Clifton to walk from the back, holding a Nalgene bottle full of what looked like Coke. Clifton stepped over the two foot wooden guard rail that marked the parking spots, leaving the mob to stand on the other side. Zach stood motionless, his arms folded across his chest, waiting to see what Clifton had in mind. Their relationship had been shaky for years, but when Clifton had chosen to live with their dad after the divorce, any chance for a brotherly friendship had been completely destroyed. They'd hardly spoken for a year.

Stopping several feet from Zach, Clifton looked over his shoulder to make sure his mob was watching. Laughing with confidence, he unscrewed the Nalgene lid and took a long drink. When his face twisted like he'd just bitten into a lemon, Zach realized that the drink in the jar was probably mixed with whiskey. Clifton laughed again, swaying and a little unsteady on his feet. His eyes fell on Rebecca, who was now holding her bike on a patch of grass about ten feet behind Zach. "Rebecca!" he called out in a loud slur that told her he'd already had too much to drink. "Congratulations on being smart!" he yelled, raising his Nalgene and toasting her honour. "It looks like you and me are cleaning up at the awards ceremony tonight. Isn't it too bad that little Zachy isn't going to be recognized? Let me see, what kind of award would they give to a momma's boy?" He laughed mockingly and took another drink, just as two of his teammates from the football team stepped over the guardrail and leaned on the cars beside him. They were all enjoying the joke and taking turns drinking from Clifton's bottle. "Zachy, why don't you have a celebration drink with your big brother?" he asked in a mocking tone. Clifton knew that Zach had never taken a drink and that he hated even the smell of booze.

As he stood listening to his brother's slurred invitations, Mr. Hiebert's proposal dropped into Zach's mind and, after a moment's deliberation, Zach decided that this was as good a time as any to test the peace response. He was fairly certain that peace wasn't going to accomplish much of anything, but he was prepared to at least toy with the idea before resorting to his usual methods of problem-solving. He wasn't afraid of Clifton and he'd already started looking over the teammates, checking for any sign of weakness. One of the things that had given him an edge in fights was his ability to study his opponents carefully. Already he'd noticed that the guy on the right was walking with a slight limp, favouring his right leg. Looks like an old football injury, Zach thought to himself. That ought to come in handy. He looked at Clifton, working hard to come up with something peaceful. OK, he said to himself finally, let's see how big brother handles this. Zach shouted loudly so the crowd could hear him, "Thanks for the offer Clifton, but I'm not thirsty. Congratulations on your award, you deserve it. You're a great athlete." Rebecca just about lost her teeth in surprise and the mob got very quiet. This was not at all what any of them had expected. Zach waited and watched, noting that a peaceful response certainly got people's attention. But what next, he wondered. It's your move, Clifton.

Clifton and his henchmen steadily and cautiously moved closer convinced that Zach was mocking them. "If you really want to congratulate me little brother, have a drink with me!" Zach took a few steps closer as well, not wanting to appear timid.

"You know I don't drink, Clifton, so why don't you just take your goons and crawl back into whatever smelly locker you jocks came out of." Zach knew this would push their buttons and immediately two angry football players were rushing him. Now I know what a quarterback feels like, he thought to himself as he tried to avoid the blitz. "So much for finding a peaceful solution," he said under his breath. The football players outweighed him and were muscular enough to hold him, dragging him like a rag doll to where Clifton stood laughing. Immediately his big brother lunged forward and with all his weight, he landed a punch on the bridge of his little brother's nose. Blood burst from Zach's face and streamed down over his mouth and onto his shirt.

As the football players dragged her friend to Clifton, Rebecca dropped her bike and began to run toward the crowd to help Zach. To do something! She was stuck in slow motion, not able to move her legs fast enough and she felt pathetically helpless, as she listened to the mob calling for Zach's blood. She screamed, as she saw Zach's head snap back, his blood spraying from his face. Rebecca was horrified and her emotions suddenly felt overwhelmed. She'd never seen anything more frightening, more violent, and more offensive in her entire life. Reaching the edge of the mob she screamed again, pushing her way through the crowd. "Leave him alone! Clifton, leave him alone! Zach! Zach!" But the blood-thirsty crowd wouldn't let her pass.

Clifton snatched a handful of his brother's hair, snapping Zach's head back so that they could look into one another's eyes. "Zachy, you hurt my feelings. I just wanted us to share a drink, to celebrate," Clifton said in a sarcastic, drunken voice. He moved his face closer now, giving Zach a strong whiff of his whiskey breath. As the pungent odor filled Zach's senses, he could feel the rage coming to life, feeding his hatred and fueling his powerful arms. There was no smell on earth that he hated more. "Hold him tight," Clifton said to his football mafia. "Here ya go, Zachy," he said with a drunken sneer. "Have a celebration sip with your big brother." The goons held Zach's head as Clifton made the mistake of pouring the drink onto Zach's face in an attempt to hit his mouth. Rebecca stood frozen, horrified, stiff as a board, furious and totally frustrated, as angry tears streamed down her face. Her hands were balled into white-knuckled fists. She simply could not believe what she was watching. And then she saw Zach's face through the crowd. Blood and drink ran down his cheeks; he was a mess. She felt nauseated. The parking lot began to spin and her breath was catching in her throat. She felt like she might pass out at any moment. She could see people cheering, but the mute button in her mind had chosen to reject the painful sounds. For Rebecca, all was confusingly silent. Drunken football players swayed and laughed. Girly groupies cheered and mocked. Clifton waved to his adoring fans, like a celebrity at the Oscars. It was all out of her control. It was happening so fast, but Rebecca was watching the play-by-play in high definition, slowly, frame by frame. All at once, the sound was back and she could hear the crowd calling to Clifton, encouraging him, challenging him to hit his brother again. But Clifton wouldn't get a second chance.

The athlete's punch had not hurt Zach as much as he was letting on and his fake defeat had confirmed to his assailants that he was indeed weak. The football goons had loosened their grips, convinced that Zach wasn't much of a threat. That was their mistake. With lightening speed, Zach lifted his right leg and brought his heel crashing down on the inside of the injured knee he'd noted earlier.

"There's one jock out for the season," he said to no one in particular, as a smile crept across his face. Even over the jeers and taunts of the crowd, the snapping of the bone sounded like a baseball launched deep into center field. The guy released his grip and melted into the ground, screaming in agony, swearing, and clutching his strangely twisted leg. With his right arm now free, Zach caught the guy on the left side off guard. Clutching a fist full of shirt with his right hand, he swung his enemy in a circle and with some momentum, threw his stunned assailant up and over the backend of a parked car. In a moment it was over, and Clifton stood alone, face-to-face with Zach.

"Yes!" Rebecca said pumping her fist in the air, as the screaming, angry spectators called for Clifton to respond. She'd never been one to enjoy any kind of violence, but Zach had just brought a big smile to her face. Little brother now stood deathly still, carefully calculating his next move. Blood dripped from his nose, his eyes burned from the drink Clifton had poured on his face, and his chest heaved from the adrenaline surge; it was Clifton's turn. Zach knew better than to lash out in anger: that's how fighters got hurt. Good fighters fought with their eyes and their brains, not with their emotions.

"First things first," Zach said under his breath, as he swatted the Nalgene from his brother's hand. It hit the ground and Zach smiled as the liquid drained from the wide-mouth jar. He waited to see how big brother would respond, but without the element of surprise or bodyguards, Clifton seemed a little short on bravery. This battle was simply going to be won by the smartest fighter and Zach knew his brother didn't have a chance. The glaring always seemed to feel longer than it actually was when you were in a fight and Zach could feel the moments ticking away, as the hatred in his brother's eyes got more intense. I don't know what he's got to be angry about, he's the one getting the award, Zach thought to himself. I'm the loser in the family, not him. One football player still lay on the ground, moaning and being comforted by a few girls. He's not going to be much of a threat, Zach thought as he searched for number two. The other guy was up from the ground, nursing a sore shoulder, and brushing dirt from his clothes. In just a moment, he'd been looking for a way through the mob to get to Zach.

Zach glanced again to see how close the other football player was and, as he looked away, Clifton jumped at his chance. The athlete of the year lunged forward swinging, but Zach had anticipated the move and he easily dropped his head, leaving Clifton nothing to hit but air. Now big brother's eyes had the look Zach had come to enjoy in a fight. It was the look of fear. Clifton's first punch hadn't done the damage he'd thought it would and his second attempt hadn't even connected. As he began to grasp the danger he was in, Clifton stumbled backward, trying to put some distance between himself and his brother. But Zach wasn't about to let him get away. It was time to see just how tough this jock really was.

Zach's knuckles were white and the beast in his chest was hungry for payback, but he would never get the chance to feed his hatred with Clifton's flesh. Before anyone knew what was happening, the athlete of the year stepped on his Nalgene and, in an instant; his drunken feet were out from under him. It wouldn't have been much of an injury had he not been so close to the parking fence, but his favorite drink had made him unsure on his feet and he came down hard, the back of his head slamming into the parking fence with a hollow thunk. Clifton's' body went limp.

For a split second the crowd stood frozen, unable to grasp this unbelievable turn of events. Then, without warning, the bloodthirsty mob scattered in a hundred different directions. Some teens went for their cars. Some ran up the alley. Others headed for the highway and out toward the mall. Some even ventured back toward the safety of the school's main doors. Everyone wanted to get away and no one came to Clifton's aid. Zach turned to see the guy he'd thrown, now dragging his friend with the bad leg over to a parked car. They were still cursing and creatively describing the things they were going to do to him. Rebecca was fighting the chaos of the scattering crowd to get to Zach, while teachers came pouring from the school like it was on fire. They were pointing and yelling and making kids sit on the little patch of grass, close to the main doors. Zach stood bleeding on himself, surprised and confused by the feeling of sadness that was settling into his heart, as he stared at his motionless brother. Somehow, seeing Clifton suffer wasn't as satisfying as Zach had thought it would be. He chuckled softly to himself, maybe Mr. Hiebert was right after all. He took a moment to rub the alcohol from his eyes with a dry corner of his shirt and he looked down to see Rebecca staring up at him. "I hate Mondays," he said with a little smile, as he brushed away the tears now running down her face. "I know what you mean," she said quietly. And she held onto him, as together they watched Mr. Edwards running toward them with a cell phone pressed to his ear. The sound of sirens was closing in on them from all directions.

~ 6 EMERGENCY ~

The oversized metallic clock was institutional issue. There was probably one just like it in every classroom in Canada, Rebecca thought to herself, as she tried to find a distraction. It was 4:35, but there was little hope that she'd be leaving any time soon. Her mind kept sneaking back to the parking lot, forcing her to watch the instant replay. Mr. Edwards had quickly brought order to a chaotic situation and in a matter of moments, teens were silently marching into the school, like a row of condemned criminals. Some of the girls were weeping softly as they shuffled arm in arm. Many of the guys walked with their heads down and all of them did their best to avoid eye contact. One of the first things Mr. Edwards had done was to separate Zach and Rebecca. He'd looked closely at Zach's injuries and then instructed him to sit up against a parked car, while Rebecca was sent to join the crowd gathering on the patch of lawn near the doors. Two other teachers trained in First Aid had quickly moved to Clifton's side to check for a pulse. Rebecca thought that they might start CPR, but they did not. Other students noted the same thing and one girl whispered, "Why don't they do something?"

A boy across from her put words to their fears, "Because he's dead, that's why. Zach killed him." The two teachers who knelt beside Clifton looked like Rebecca had felt only moments ago: scared and helpless. There was nothing that any of them could do, but sit and wait for the ambulance.

Tired of watching the clock, Rebecca shifted her attention to the window. Again her mind wandered, this time to the image of the

Emergency Medical Technicians, or EMTs, as it said on their orange vests. They had moved quickly, knowing exactly what they needed from the truck and how to best divide their attention. While a woman moved to assist Zach, three other EMTs knelt beside Clifton. Recognizing that the students were still sitting on the grass, Mr. Edwards had ordered the teachers to take them inside to give Zach and Clifton some privacy. It was that final image of Zach sitting on the gravel holding something on his face as a police officer stood by, that now stuck in Rebecca's mind. She wondered what would happen to him. She had no idea when she would see him again.

~

As Rebecca sat lost in thought at her desk, Zach sat in the gravel with an ice pack on his nose, watching carefully as the EMTs fastened a white collar around his brother's neck. It just didn't seem right. For as long as he could remember Zach had wanted Clifton to suffer, even to die. One would think that this would be a time of celebration and triumph. Finally Zach's violent fantasy had come true. But as his brother lay motionless in the gravel, Zach's mind was forcing him back in time. He closed his eyes and listened to the giggling little voices. Slowly the scene came into view. It was two brothers having a bath. They were covered in white foamy bubbles and there was water all over the floor. They were making waves and laughing themselves silly. In those days, he'd loved everything about his big brother. He'd wanted to dress like him, to walk like him, and to break the rules just like Clifton. Now, for the first time in years, it was all coming back to him and Zach opened his eyes to the surprise of a tear running down his left cheek. How had it come to this, when secretly his big brother had been his hero?

Cautiously, the EMTs moved Clifton onto a flat board and quickly carried him to the waiting ambulance. The tech working on Zach cleaned his nose and face and encouraged him to go to the hospital for an x-ray. Then both rescue trucks were gone and Zach was left with Mr. Edwards and two police officers, all eager to interrogate him. The officers asked Zach how much he'd had to drink and were surprised, even a little amused, when he'd said he didn't drink alcohol. "Just another bad lie from another stupid kid," muttered the officer who walked over to his car shaking his head.

The officer who remained by Zach's side said, "Son, I'd like you to tilt your head way back and stretch your arms out to your sides like this." The cop demonstrated and Zach copied his movements. "Good. Now using your left hand, I'd like you to touch the tip of your nose. And now the right hand." Zach's balance was steady and it left the officers a little baffled, given that he smelled like he'd been bathing in whiskey all afternoon. "Now I'd like you to walk toward me, arms straight out from your sides, one foot in front of the other, until I tell you to stop." Again, the officers were confused with the mixed messages they were getting. Something didn't add up. Finally, Zach was asked to blow hard into a tube attached to a small box about the size of a cigarette pack and instantly all three adults were shocked. Zach had been telling the truth: there was no sign of alcohol in his system.

~

"Rebecca, it's your turn," said the teacher who had just entered the room. But Rebecca was a hundred miles away, still stuck on the image of Zach with the ice pack on his face. Still frozen on the body that lay in the dirt. Still unable to stop the crowd's blood-chant from filling her ears. Simply unable to turn it off. Not liking being ignored, the teacher made her way across the room, drawing glares from some of the students sitting at their desks "Rebecca!" she said in a loud voice.

Frightened by the sound, Rebecca jumped and then snapped, "What's your problem?" she said with a good deal of attitude. "Why are you yelling at me? Why is everyone so angry? What's wrong with you people?" she said looking around at the room full of stone-faced teens. Rebecca wasn't crying. She felt more like a dry stick slowly being bent beyond its breaking point. She was angry. Her frustration level was high and her patience was thin.

Remembering that the student had just been through a traumatic situation, the teacher quickly changed her posture and her tone of voice. "I'm sorry I startled you, Rebecca. I'm not angry with you. Please come with me to Mr. Edward's office. It's your turn." Rebecca gathered her things and followed the teacher out of the room and down the hall. She was thankful that she'd already had an opportunity to call her parents. One by one they'd all been given the choice and when it had come to Rebecca, she'd ended up with an answering machine. In a few hours, she would discover that her mom had been busy with a client and that she too had called the machine, asking Rebecca to meet her at the school at 6:30. And her dad had completely forgotten about a meeting that he needed to attend. His message said that he'd meet her at the school shortly after 6. Her mind was so foggy and scatterbrained that she completely forgot about her mom's cell phone. For now, she was on her own. Poor Dexter, she thought to herself, as she walked down the hall thinking about her dog's scheduled potty break. He's not going to be too happy with me.

The teacher opened the door allowing Rebecca to walk into the room full of serious faces and notepads. Mr. Edwards sat on the right and a female police officer on the left. "Hey, Rebecca," Mr. Edwards said like he was greeting an old friend. "Please have a seat, this won't take long. I know that this has been a difficult day for you, but we need you to help us understand what happened out there in the parking lot. Can you do that?" he asked.

"Yes, I think so," Rebecca responded in a quiet and hesitant voice.

"This is Officer Preston and she needs to ask you a few questions." Rebecca agreed and took her seat, watching with some fascination as the officer directed her questions in precise, robotic, emotionless tones. This woman is an ice queen, Rebecca thought to herself as the interview continued.

"Mr. Edwards tells me that you had a conversation with Zach early this morning. I'll need you to provide me with the details of that conversation." That was a command Rebecca had not expected and one she certainly had no intention of obeying. Zach had opened his heart and had shared things with her that he'd never told anyone, and it was her responsibility to keep his privacy sacred. Rebecca folded her arms across her chest and leaned back in her chair.

"I don't see how our conversation has anything to do with the fight," she said in a matter of fact tone.

"You can let me be the judge of that. What did you talk about?" the officer commanded for a second time.

But Rebecca was in no mood to be pushed. "We talked about

Zach's life," she said through gritted teeth.

"I'll need the details of that discussion," the officer said, straightening her back to demonstrate her authority and to intimidate her witness.

"What we talked about is private. It had nothing to do with Clifton or the fight," Rebecca said again, this time with more force. But Officer Preston wasn't prepared to be outmaneuvered by a disrespectful teenager.

"Rebecca I will need your *full* cooperation and if I do not get it, I will charge you for interfering with a criminal investigation and you will go to jail. Am I making myself clear?" In an instant, Rebecca was on her feet, transformed from a gentle girl, into an angry woman. Both adults were caught off guard and immediately Officer Preston was at attention, her face close to Rebecca's.

"Criminal investigation? Against Zach? He was attacked by three guys! Two held him while Clifton hit him. Didn't you see the blood on Zach's face? They poured alcohol all over his head and if he hadn't fought back . . . Clifton was trying to kill him! Who's the criminal here?" Rebecca sat down exasperated and a little embarrassed by her outburst. She just wanted to go home. She could tell that she was not fully in control of herself and that her emotions were rubbed thin. "I'm sorry," she said again in her gentle voice. "I'm not usually like this. It's just that, I've never seen a real fight. I don't feel well." Placing her hands on the table in front of her to stop her room from spinning, Rebecca took hold of herself. Inhaling deeply, she blew out the air with a sigh. When she looked up, it was Mr. Edwards she spoke to. She was working hard now to avoid Officer Preston's ice-cold eyes. "I talked with Zach about his dad," she said quietly. "And about his dad's drinking problem. That's why Zach doesn't drink. That's why he freaked out when Clifton emptied the Nalgene on his face. He told me his dad hits him." As soon as the words fell from her lips, Rebecca began to feel a deep sense of shame wash over her. Zach's most precious secrets had just slipped out and her betrayal left her red in the face and feeling like she'd broken his trust. But she needed to say something to help them to understand. Zach wasn't the criminal here: he was the victim.

The parking lot was quiet and almost empty as Rebecca stepped out the back doors in search of her bike. "What a day," she said to herself as once again she gulped down the fresh spring air. She paused for just a moment to gather her thoughts. The last time she'd enjoyed a moment of fresh, cool air she had just closed the back door to the veterinary hospital. She smiled as she thought about Mason and instantly her brain jumped to Dexter. "Oh Dexter, I hope you don't hate me," she said out loud as she wondered how long he'd be able to wait for his bathroom break. Rebecca picked her bike up off the grass where she'd dropped it, surprised that it was still there. She'd already had one bike stolen, but that one had been locked. "Maybe I should just lay my bike on the grass from now on," she said smiling and shaking her head. "Maybe bike thieves pride themselves on the challenge of breaking my locks." Riding toward the main driveway, Rebecca was finally on her way home. As she neared the sidewalk, she could hear a car racing down the alley behind her. She turned in time to see a small red Toyota slide sideways on the gravel lot, stopping to park on an odd angle. The driver jumped from the car and began running toward the back doors of the school. "Oh no," Rebecca said with a gasp, "this can't be good." As soon as the driver had jumped from the car, Rebecca had recognized her as Clifton's girlfriend, Alisa. And by the looks of things, she'd just heard the news. Rebecca turned her bike sharply and called out in a loud voice, "Alisa! Alisa, wait!" Even from a small distance, Rebecca could see the look of dread on the girl's face and, as she got closer, she could tell that Alisa had been crying. Setting her bike on the stand, the two girls embraced. They'd been friends for years and this wasn't the first time that Alisa had turned to Rebecca for help.

"Clifton's dead!" Alisa said in a voice bordering on hysterics. "Rebecca, how could this happen? How could he get killed? How could he do this to me now of all times? It's not fair! Not now when I need him the most." Holding her for a long moment, Rebecca tried to help Alisa calm down.

"Who told you that Clifton was dead?" she asked in a steady voice.

"I got a call on my cell at work. It was Matt. He said he was at a fight and that he'd gotten away when the teachers came out. He told me that he saw Zach kill Clifton." She began to loose control, her tears pouring down her cheeks, and her legs giving out beneath her. In a moment, the two girls were on their knees, embracing, and Rebecca was busy wondering if the news she'd just heard was true.

"Alisa, hold on. We've got to think this through. I was at the fight too," she said, as Alisa looked up in surprise.

"You were at a fight?" she said in surprise.

"Yes. It's a long story. Anyway, let me tell you what I saw." And with that Rebecca gave Alisa a detailed account of the event. How the crowd cornered Zach. How Clifton had been drunk and how he'd turned his football friends loose on his brother. She told about the punch and the alcohol poured on Zach's face. She explained how Zach had defended himself, and finally she'd described Clifton's fall and the injury to the back of his head. "When the EMTs were here, I saw them checking his pulse and rushing to get him into the back of the ambulance. They seemed to be working quickly. I don't think they would have done all of that if Clifton was dead." Alisa listened carefully, weeping softly, and feeling sick to her stomach that Clifton could act like such a monster. She was embarrassed, but it felt good to have some hope that he might still be alive. "Alisa, I heard some teachers talking in the hall before I left. They said he'd been taken to the Health Sciences Hospital. Why don't we jump in your car and go over together, maybe we can get someone to tell us how he's doing." In a flash, Rebecca had forgotten about Dexter and her parents and the banquet. All that mattered now was helping her friend.

The emergency waiting room was chaotic and the two girls were immediately disappointed. When they'd asked for details about their friend, they'd been told that Clifton had been brought in and that he was in intensive care. All other information was private and would be given to family members only. Rebecca kicked herself for getting Alisa's hopes up. She should have known better. She knew through her work at the animal hospital that there were tight restrictions on who could receive information about patients, even when the patient was an animal. "Why don't we wait for a bit, I'll bet Clifton's mom and dad have been called. They'll probably be here any minute and then we can find out how he's doing," Rebecca said. As they sat watching the room, listening to the sounds of suffering, Alisa's words began to recycle through Rebecca's mind. Something Alisa had said back at the school had sounded strange. What was it? Rebecca searched her memory files for the words. After a few moments of searching, her memory finally delivered Alisa's words: "How could this happen to me, now of all times? Now when I need him the most." Just as Rebecca began to ponder what the words might mean, Alisa was getting ready to break the silence.

"Rebecca," she paused for a moment, looking down at the grey hospital tile. "Can I tell you something?" She looked into Rebecca's eyes to test her friend's non-verbal response. But Rebecca had heard this question a hundred times before from a hundred different people and it was always a no-brainer for her to answer.

"Of course you can, what is it?" She could tell that Alisa was carrying a weight, some secret that she needed to confess. "Alisa, I'm your friend. Let me help you."

Without a moment's hesitation, Alisa blurted out the words she'd needed to say to someone for two months: "I'm having Clifton's baby."

~

While the two girls sat in the emergency room talking, Rebecca's parents were nervously pacing the tile floor of the high school gymnasium surrounded by smiling award winners and their parents. It was so unlike Rebecca to do something like this and that fact fueled their parental paranoia. Something awful must have happened. Images of abduction, of kidnapping, of horrible things that only parents can conjure up filled their minds. Neither of them had been home yet, so there was a chance that she was at the house. But Rebecca's dad had called and there had been no answer. He'd thought about retrieving the messages from the machine, but Rebecca was the only one who knew the remote access code. To confuse matters more, Rebecca's dad had spotted her bike as he'd headed toward the back doors of the school. Strangely, it was down the alley toward the road and it had been unlocked and propped up on its stand. As hard as he'd tried, he just could not come up with a good reason for her bike to be unlocked and half way down the alley. He was trying hard to stay calm, but his sense of dread was growing with every minute. Rebecca's parents sat across from one another during the dinner, their eyes meeting throughout the evening, their hands touching. With the others around the table celebrating, there was no opportunity for them to put words to their feelings. They were afraid and the empty chair at the table constantly reminded them that they had good reason to be. As the awards banquet got underway, Rebecca's mom moved to the platform to sit with the other board members. It was her job to present the award to the outstanding athlete of the year. She had been told to read the description of the award, to read the name of the winner, and to receive the award on his behalf. Figuring that Clifton was ill, she agreed to follow the same procedure they'd used almost every year, only this time she would accept his award and return to her seat.

~

As Rebecca's mom stood to present the award, Zach stood to pace the floor of his tiny prison cell. He looked over the steel-framed cot at the etchings in the wall, signatures of former visitors, no doubt. He stared at the blue ink staining the ends of his finger tips, a reminder of the fingerprinting process and the interrogation. He was in a prison cell waiting for someone to come to their senses. As far as he could tell, he hadn't committed a crime, but he did understand that it would take some time to sort things out. He snickered a little to himself. If he'd been the first cop on the scene, he'd have been pretty suspicious too. A teenager stinking of whiskey, covered in blood, and standing over a lifeless body. If that didn't say guilty, Zach didn't know what would. He sat down again on his cot and thought about Clifton, but his mind quickly turned to his mom. He'd been allowed to call her, but there had been no answer. He'd left a message. If she was working a double-shift, Zach knew that his message would be orphaned until morning. "What would happen to her?" he wondered, if he had to stay in prison. And now more questions began to gnaw at him. Would she slip back into depression? Would she quit her job and crawl back into bed? Who would take care of her if he was stuck in a cell? What would she do if Clifton died? Suddenly it dawned on him that she might blame him for what happened. That she might reject him just as his dad had done. This took Zach's breath away as he paced in his confined space. The thought of living life without her paralyzed him for a moment and in an instant, he found himself hoping for Clifton's full recovery. He'd probably just been knocked out, Zach thought to himself with some confidence. He'd seen it happen in a few fights; it was normal. They'd look him over at the hospital and send him home with a headache. It was nothing to worry about. Zach sat down smiling as he thought about the pounding headache Clifton would have when he woke up. It was bad enough that he'd smacked his head on the fence, but with all that alcohol in his system, he was bound to have a killer hangover as well. "Serves him right for drinking and fighting," Zach said to his four cell walls, working to find something amusing about his situation.

But right at that moment, as he sat on his cot convincing himself that Clifton's injury would lead to nothing more than a bad headache, his mom sat in a tiny hospital room with a few friends, softly weeping to herself and asking anyone who would listen, "Why Clifton? Why?"

~ 7 OVERWHELMED ~

"**D**ad! Mom!" Rebecca yelled with surprise as she ran across the sterile waiting room. In her parent's arms, she found the comfort, safety, and strength she'd so often taken for granted. Finally, someone who would care for her. Locked in their embrace and in that sacred space of family, the strength Rebecca had summoned finally dissolved into tears. From the early hours of her day, Rebecca had been caring for others. She'd been strong for Zach, listening to his story and being present with him as he emptied his garbage can of secrets. She'd listened, as Amy told her that life wasn't worth living and she'd been a support for Alisa when she'd found out about the baby. She'd weathered a blood-thirsty mob, an ice-queen, a disappointed math mentor, an evil English teacher, and a vice-principal – twice. It had been such a long day. As her parent's held her, she realized just how much she needed their strength. They held onto each other for a long time. And they cried, and laughed, and squeezed each other tight. Her parents could not remember a time when they had felt such relief.

As they sat on the emergency room chairs, Rebecca began to explain how she'd remembered to call her mom's cell phone later in the evening. "Was your phone on, Mom?" she asked.

Her mom looked at her and smiled, brushing her little girl's hair back from her face. "No, Rebecca. I had to turn my phone off for the awards ceremony. I'm so sorry you couldn't get through to me." When Rebecca asked her dad how they'd found her, he began to tell his side of the story. He told her how strange it had been to see her bike in the alley and how, after the banquet, he was on his way to load it into the trunk of his car, when Mr. Edwards had caught them and asked for a few moments to talk. As he led them toward his office, Mr. Edward's had mentioned that he'd not seen Clifton's dad at the banquet and wondered if either of them had seen him.

As Zach's mom listened to the story, she dropped her head in shame. "He was supposed to be there," she said quietly. "I had to work, I couldn't get the time off. He promised me he'd be there." Rebecca's mom reached over to take hold of her hand and Rebecca's dad continued.

"The vice-principal told us all about the fight and explained what he knew of Rebecca's involvement. When he was done, we asked him which hospital Clifton had been taken to. He didn't know if you'd be here, but we thought it was worth a shot," Rebecca's dad said as he gave his little girl another gentle squeeze.

With her dad's story finished, Rebecca began to recount the events of her day, beginning with the fight. Zach's mom was eager to hear the details of her son's accident; she still didn't understand exactly how the injury had happened. Rebecca told the story with care and was beginning to describe how Zach defended himself, when they heard a tenor voice calling out for Mrs. Turner. Zach's mom raised her hand and a man in a white lab coat made his way across the room toward them. "Mrs. Turner?"

"Yes, well no. I'm divorced. I go by Miss McNabb now – Teresa McNabb." "Miss McNabb, I'm Dr. Rand. Could we speak in private?"

"Doctor please tell me, how is Clifton? Is he going to be OK? When can we talk to him?" Zach's mom fired questions at the doctor with panic in her voice.

"That's what I'd like to speak with you about. Perhaps we could move to one of the private rooms down the hall."

"I'd like my friends to be with me, if that's alright," she said holding on to Alisa's arm. The doctor agreed and together the group moved down the hallway toward a room. Once they were all seated and the door had been closed, Dr. Rand pulled an x-ray from a brown folder he'd been carrying. Hooking the picture to a lighted board mounted on the wall, everyone could see the news before the doctor had said a word. The image revealed a clear break in Clifton's neck. The doctor looked over at Zach's mom.

"To use plain English, your son has broken his neck. But there's something else you need to know. Miss McNabb, your son has slipped into a coma." The room was silent as the news drained the color from their faces. The doctor took the time to carefully explain the medical details and Rebecca was struck by his empathy and compassion. "To be honest, I don't know what to tell you. He could stay in that coma for an hour, or for a year. You need to understand that the damage to his spinal cord has been severe."

"How severe? What does that mean?" she said trying to understand the image on the x-ray.

"It means that, if your son comes out of the coma, he will be confined to a wheelchair for the rest of his life. Miss McNabb, Clifton will never have the use of his arms or his legs."

"He'll be a quadriplegic?" Alisa said slowly, horrified by the words that now spilled from her mouth.

"Yes, that's correct. I am sorry," the doctor replied, fighting to control his own emotional response.

"No! That can't be. Clifton's winning the athletic award this year," said Zach's mom as her voice began to quiver and shake. She stood absent-mindedly and began to pace the floor, nervously talking out loud, but not to anyone in particular. "He's going to play football. He's a good boy. We'll get him the best help money can buy. I'll get another job. We'll take him to the States. We can beat this."

"Miss McNabb, I'm sorry, but Clifton will never recover." It sounded cruel, but even Rebecca understood that the doctor's words were necessary. He could not lead her to believe that there was any hope.

"No. It's not fair!" she cried in despair. "My baby. My little boy," and with those words she dropped to a chair, put her hands to her face, and wept with the agony that only a mother can feel. Rebecca's mom pulled her own chair close and quickly embraced Zach's mom, rocking her slowly, brushing the hair from her eyes, and providing tissue. But she was careful not to fill the air with empty words of hope. There simply was no hope. This was a time for silence.

Rebecca and Alisa were staggered by the news. They simply could not believe what they were hearing. When their eyes finally dared to meet in that tiny room, they did not speak, but each knew the question burning in the other's mind: What would happen to the baby? Alisa raised her hands to her mouth. Clifton will never hold our baby, she thought to herself as she began to sob. Rebecca could not move, but her father reached for Alisa and pulled her close. Months later, Rebecca would describe these difficult moments as "something that was happening to someone else." The situation had so overwhelmed her ability to cope that her feelings had been baffled. Not a single emotion had stepped forward to take the job of supplying a feeling; there was nothing but numbness. Waves of new thoughts crashed into her, knocking her around, threatening her safety. Clifton will be in a wheelchair for the rest of his life. He'll never teach his little girl to walk, or to ride a bike, or to play soccer. He'll never hold Alisa's hand, or give her a back rub, or push a stroller. It was by far the saddest news that Rebecca had ever heard, but she'd come to the end of her ability to care. She was finished. Spent. Used up and shut down. All cared out. She sat down slowly, not realizing that her face had turned white and that her hands had begun to shake. She could not speak, or feel, or think, or care. She simply sat very still as the current of her mind pulled her mercilessly into the rapids of her thoughts. What would Alisa do now? Would she have the baby? Would she give the baby up for adoption? Would she get an abortion? Would she marry Clifton and take care of him and their baby? She was only 17. How could she make enough money to support a family? And what about university? Alisa was considering a career in business. What would happen to her dreams now? How could she possibly handle all this pressure? It just wasn't fair!

Dr. Rand had been quiet for a few moments, wanting to give everyone time to process what he'd just said. "I'm sorry, Miss McNabb. I wish I had better news for you. I can take you in to see your son, but the others will have to remain in the waiting room. Just let the nurse know when you're ready." And with that, he excused himself and they were left to sit with their grief.

PART II

THE UNEXPECTED COST
OF CARING

~ 8 BLACK OUT ~

The joy her parents had experienced finding their daughter in the emergency room at the Health Sciences Center was nothing compared to the celebration waiting in the mud room at home, as Rebecca pushed the back door open to a pair of eager brown eyes. "I'm sorry fella," she said as she opened the door to let him pass. But dogs understand forgiveness and friendship better than most humans, and Dexter was no exception. As Rebecca sat down on the thick den carpet, her dog came wiggling into the room, quickly throwing himself to the floor, and rolling onto his back hoping for a good dose of much needed attention. His girl sat very still, watching her upside down dog wag his tail, while her dad put his coat in the closet and her mom checked the machine for messages. "Alright," Rebecca said, giving in to the irresistible smile.

When her dad finally came into the room, Dexter was enjoying a full body massage. Strolling casually into the den, he stretched and yawned and looked at their grandfather clock in surprise, "12:30 in the morning? How can it be 12:30 already? What a day." Standing near the fireplace, he looked again at the daughter he'd thought he'd lost. Images of Rebecca in a wheelchair, unable to touch her dog, filled his mind. "Why is it that as soon as you have a child your brain develops the ability to create worst case scenarios?" he said as his wife came into the room.

"You mean like freaking out every time I don't call home," Rebecca said without looking up.

"Yeah, something like that," he said stretching again.

"Becky honey, it's been a long day. Why don't you get up to bed?

I'm sure you must be exhausted." Rebecca looked at her mom, refusing to believe that this woman was stupid. She sat on the parent's advisory council at the school, managed a home, and had a successful career in real estate. No doubt she knew every one of her co-workers and clients by name. How was it then that she could not get her own daughter's name right?

"What is wrong with you?" she asked her mom in a voice that only a teenager could create.

"What do you mean, dear?" She had no idea what Rebecca was talking about. "Do you have a metal plate in your head? Have you got that forgetting disease that old people get? What's it called?"

"You mean Alzheimer's? No, I don't have Alzheimer's, dear. What's the problem, Becky?" her mom said in a tired voice. Rebecca stood squeezing her arms to her side and balling her hands into small white-knuckled fists.

"You are so frustrating. How do you stay married to this woman?" she asked her dad as her anger began to burn. Her dad thought for a moment and started to reply, but about two words into his explanation he'd caught sight of his wife's eyes. Perhaps silence was the best choice for now, he reasoned correctly. "The problem, Mother, is that months ago we decided that you would stop calling me Becky. I've had enough! My name is Re-be-cca. Get 'Hooked On Phonics' Mom. Say it with me: Re-be-cca. Is this something you can manage or should we hire an educational assistant to help you?" Rebecca had never spoken to her parents like this before and, for a moment; neither of them had a clue how to respond. They'd heard stories from other parents about angry, door-slamming teenagers, but they'd never been able to relate. Rebecca had always been kind and gracious and she'd never had much of a temper. Up until that moment, parenting her had been simple.

"You're tired, dear. It's been a hard day. Why don't you go up to bed and we can discuss this in the morning."

"Dammit Mom, I want to discuss it now. Right now! I want to hear you say it. I want to hear you promise me that you will never call me Becky again. Right now!" Rebecca waved her arms like a criminal lawyer caught up in the closing arguments of a high profile case. But Rebecca was coming dangerously close to unleashing her mother's temper.

"Listen Rebecca, you're making a big deal out of nothing. Now get to bed before this becomes a problem."

But their little girl wasn't finished. "It's not a big deal about nothing, it's my name! Now promise me!" There was a long pause as her mother sat, considering the irony of the moment. Only a few hours had passed since she'd felt the overwhelming joy of finding this little girl who had now morphed into a parent-eating monster. It had been so hard to let her little freckly-faced Becky grow up, but now it was time to let go. Rebecca's mom stood, feeling the kind of sadness that only a parent can understand, and she said goodbye to her little girl and accepted a young woman into her home.

"If it's that important to you Rebecca then yes, I will promise you. I will not call you Becky. Now if you'll excuse me, it's been a difficult day, I need to get some sleep." And with that Rebecca's mom disappeared up the stairs.

Rebecca's dad had no idea how to patch things up and settled instead for a cup of tea and a cookie. Rebecca was sitting on the carpet beside Dexter, feeling awful about the way she'd just treated her mom. "What a rotten day," she said to herself under her breath. She looked up at her dad as he unbuckled his black leather belt to relax and slowly pulled it through the loops. She could hear the sound of cloth on leather and, for some reason, her hands began to shake. She could feel moisture beading on her forehead and fear gripping her by the throat as her stomach twisted. She looked up at the safest man she knew and she was filled with fear and hatred. Suddenly, the room was turning and tilting and spinning out of control. She grabbed the arm of the couch, trying to pull herself to the cushion, but now her breathing had become rapid and her legs could no longer support her. She gulped for air and both hands rose to her chest in an expression of panic. She couldn't slow down, she couldn't breathe. Rebecca was going to die. Before her world turned to black, she thought she heard hollow, shadowy voices somewhere off in the distance. Someone calling. Maybe it was her name, she couldn't tell. She felt strong arms holding her, lifting her, supporting her. But she had no idea where she was. For some reason, her body had betrayed her; she was completely out of control, and neither Rebecca, nor her parents, had any idea why.

~

"You little puke."

"I mean it if you tell anyone, I'll do it. I'll kill myself and it'll be your fault."

"I'm having his baby. Rebecca, help me, I'm having Clifton's baby."

"Come on, have a drink with your big brother."

"He'll never be able to use his hands or his feet. He'll never hold his baby."

"Some day you'll thank me for teaching you how to be a real man."

"Let him go. Clifton let him go!"

"No problem, Rebecca, all you had to do was ask. You know I'd never do anything to hurt my little brother." The scene turned dark and thunder clouds rolled over the parking lot. It started to pour and Rebecca could feel the large drops of rain pounding against her skin. Clifton was soaking wet. He slowly drew a knife from inside his coat and starting walking toward his brother. Zach was trying to free himself from two faceless athletes.

"No Clifton, you can't do this," she screamed. But instead of stopping, he simply shot her an evil grin, as he raised his knife to attack. As the parking lot faded to black, Rebecca saw herself walking inside an old barn. There was no sign of Amy, but her voice came from somewhere close by.

"Keep this chain to remember what you did to me Rebecca."

"Amy, where are you? Amy, you don't have to do this. I never told anyone. Amy, I never told!"

There was hay in the loft and pigeons cooed in the rafters. Right in front of her, hanging from one of the rafters, was a long, frayed rope with a loop in the end. "Amy, you don't have to do this," she called, feeling sick with panic and dread. But there was no answer and no sign of her friend. Just a feeling that something terrible was about to happen. All at once, the scene changed again and she was back in her own bedroom. Rebecca could feel herself out of breath, like she'd been running. She heard the door open and turned to see her dad holding a Nalgene bottle full of dark liquid.

"Why don't you and I have a little drink?"

"Dad? No, I don't want to drink with you." Stepping backward she began to shake as he entered her room and closed her door.

"You've always been a disappointment to me, Rebecca. I need to teach you how to be strong." He began unlatching his belt and sliding it through the loops. "This belt should toughen you up. One day you're gonna thank me for this."

"No!" she gasped as Rebecca sat straight up in her bed covered in sweat. She looked around taking a few moments to get her bearings. The room was empty, lit only by the glow from her computer monitor. The blankets were thrown to the floor and her sweat-soaked hair was matted to her face. She had no idea what had happened to her or how she'd gotten to her bed. Fear still tingled on her shoulder blades but, after a few moments, Rebecca knew that she had nothing to fear. She was home. She was in her own bed. It had been a nightmare.

Having washed her face and neck with cool water, Rebecca's mind cleared. What time is it, she wondered as she reached for her alarm clock. "4:45 in the morning," she grumbled, lying back on the bed with a grunt. It's the day that wouldn't die, she thought to herself as she lay staring at her bedroom ceiling. For a few moments she enjoyed just lying still, listening to her own breath, and the sounds of a few early birds, waking up just outside of her window. But the imprint of the previous day's conversations would not let her rest. She wondered where Zach was and fought the urge to call him right then and there. Amy was probably at home, but Rebecca wondered how she would patch things up enough to be a support for her during this difficult time. First things first: tomorrow morning she'd have to contact Alisa and begin creating a support system to help her make some decisions about her pregnancy. "So many needs, so little energy left," she said to herself as she drifted back to sleep.

She woke with a jump, like someone had poked her, and quickly recognized the press of warm, bad breath gently huffing on the left side of her head. She turned to see her most adoring fan on her bed, staring at her with spirited eyes and urging her to join in life's highest calling. Play? Rebecca turned and buried her head under her pillow, "Go away Dexter," she said unconvincingly. Hearing her voice, her dad popped his head in to see how she was doing. Rebecca's eyes caught her alarm clock and she bolted to a sitting position. "It's 10 o'clock! Why didn't you wake me? I've got school stuff that has to be done today."

"Hold on there sport," her dad said as he gently pressed her shoulder blades back down into her bed. "You're not going anywhere this morning. You had a rough day yesterday and your mom and I both thought you could use a little extra rest. When you get up, I'll make you some brunch." Her dad moved to open her curtains to let the sunshine flood the bedroom. "Now I know you may not be crazy about this Rebecca, but your mother's been able to get you an appointment to see a counselor this afternoon. Mr. Edwards thought it might be helpful after all you've been through, and we agree."

"A counselor? What for? There's nothing wrong with me. I'm fine. I was just exhausted last night, that's all. I just needed a good night's rest." Of course, she was smart enough to know that it wouldn't be to her advantage to admit that she hadn't actually had a good night's rest.

"Sorry kiddo, we've already made the appointment. Think of it as a mental health checkup. Forty-five minutes, clean bill of health, and you're out of there." He smiled, but Rebecca was glaring at him suspiciously. "What?" he said in an innocent voice. "Come on. Get dressed and I'll make you some breakfast." And with that, he was out her door and down the stairs with Dexter at his heels.

~ 9 DISORIENTED ~

"Rebecca! I am so glad I found you. This whole day has been stupid and yesterday was awful. You've got no idea how hard my life is. I really need somebody to talk to. Let's get a table in the caf, we've got about half an hour before next class."

"Yeah, sure Shae," Rebecca replied with a casual smile. After brunch, Rebecca had managed to convince her dad that a few hours at school wouldn't kill her, that she was fine. Besides, after missing part of yesterday, she didn't want to press her luck with some of the less gracious teachers. But now, as she stood in the hallway, face to face with Shae, Rebecca wished she'd stayed home. Walking into the cafeteria, Shae sat with her back facing the same table that Rebecca and Amy had sat at yesterday. It was where Rebecca had heard that her best friend was going to kill herself. It was the place where she'd received a gold chain. The table where she'd failed Amy. She'd wanted to avoid the cafeteria today She didn't want to run into Amy and she just couldn't stomach going back to the table where they'd talked. "So much for staying away from the caf today," she said under her breath as she took her seat.

"So, I was talking with Steve and he is so not over Shelley. I totally knew that he still liked her. And I talked with her yesterday and she says she might get back with him, but she wants to make him suffer for a little while. I think he's kind of below her, but he's not a total loser. She's so cool though and I know she could get any guy . . . Rebecca are you even listening to me?"

"What, oh sure yeah, she's cool," said Rebecca nodding her head and trying not to look at the table across from them. As Shae chatted on, Rebecca's mind continually wandered, she couldn't seem to focus her attention on her friend's words. She wondered where Amy was and she found herself scanning the room to see if she might spot her. She wondered if Alisa was with Clifton and if Zach was home, or in prison, or at school. As her eyes wandered over the sea of faces, she spotted a few who had been at the fight. None of them would look at her and, as Rebecca's eyes burned holes in them, her throat tightened, her mind playing the footage of a blood-thirsty mob screaming and chanting for more. It made her feel sick and it was all she could do to contain herself. A part of her wanted to hunt down every kid that had been a part of that mob and tell them what idiots they'd been.

Shae hadn't seemed to notice that Rebecca was a million miles away, but she did get her attention when she mentioned the fight. "So did you hear about the fight yesterday? Zach is in serious trouble for trying to kill his brother. That guy is such a psycho." Shae always had contempt in her voice when she spoke about Zach. It had only been a few months since her ex-boyfriend had been stupid enough to challenge him, only to wind up with a number of unwanted injuries including a dark blue eye and a severely wounded ego. Shae hated her ex, but for some strange reason she also hated Zach for what he'd done. She'd hardly finished her sentence before Rebecca was on her feet, angry and red in the face.

"Zach is not a psycho and I suggest you keep your mouth shut until you have your facts straight." And with that, Rebecca picked up her pack and began to walk toward the door.

"Wow, what's with you? It's not like he's your boyfriend," she said with a disgusted laugh. Rebecca was only a table away when Shae's words hit her like a brick in the back of the head. Dropping her pack, she turned and her friend could see that she'd pushed the wrong button. She'd never seen Rebecca mad, no one had really. She was always controlled and compassionate, but her reputation was about to change. Shae was standing as Rebecca approached and, for a moment, the two stood face to face. Having seen Rebecca toss her bag on the ground and turn quickly, teens at nearby tables stopped their conversations, waiting to see if there might be a fight.

"I am so sick of your irritating emotional drama and your insensitivity toward other people's feelings," Rebecca spat. "All you care about is your own little insignificant world." Shae was stunned.

Rebecca had always been her friend. She'd listened when no one else would and Shae had never heard her speak a harsh word to anyone.

"Well, if my world is so insignificant, I guess I won't waste any more of your time talking about it. I'll just go live my insignificant life somewhere else." And with a toss of her red hair, Shae grabbed her backpack, turned, and headed for the doors.

Disappointed that the argument hadn't produced a fight, people in the crowd began to gather their trays and packs for class. After she'd watched Shae storm off, Rebecca turned to look again at the table where she and Amy had sat and she was filled with sadness. As she gently lowered herself into a cafeteria chair, that unstoppable reel began to play again. Amy was going away, but she wasn't moving to Calgary. "How could I have been so stupid?" she said to herself quietly. "How could I let her just walk away without doing something to help her?" As soon as the question hit her mind, Rebecca's inside voice turned cynical. Help? Like I know anything about helping people. Mr. Edwards was right. I need to worry about myself and let people take their problems to trained professionals. I stink at helping. The words stung, but Rebecca could not remember ever saying anything to herself that seemed truer than those words in that moment at that table. And her condemning attitude wasn't about to quit, it was just getting warmed up. "Let me see. I tell Shae that her life is insignificant. That was helpful, wasn't it?" she said quietly, sadness now dripping from her voice. "You took Amy's gold chain and she walked off to kill herself. That was some pretty effective helping, too." Rebecca was surrounded by people in the cafeteria, but she felt marooned with her accusing thoughts, banished to some isolated island to live with the memories of her failures. "You thought you helped Zach and look what happened to him. The truth is that everyone I've tried to help has ended up in worse shape." She hung her head in shame trying hard not to believe these thoughts. Had all her helping really been so bad? Had she hurt the people she'd wanted to help?

As she sat with these painful questions, Rebecca reached up to rub the stress knots from the right side of her neck. The questions stopped assaulting her, but one final, knockout punch had settled in the center of her chest. "If my caring only hurts others then I guess . . ." She could barely get herself to say the words out loud. They were heavy and slowed her speech as she mumbled to herself words she'd never dreamed she could say. But they had to be spoken. Rebecca could no longer connect with people and, with the help of her cynical thoughts, she was losing her grasp on hope. Her worst nightmare had become a reality: her efforts had been meaningless and she'd failed to help those who'd trusted her to listen. Finally, she spoke what was in her heart, "If my caring only hurts others then I guess it's time to stop caring." Cynicism like a schoolyard bully, always attacks in weakness. Rebecca would never have put up with this kind of talk from anyone else, but her own poorly behaved thoughts were getting away with convincing a strong, brilliant, compassionate woman that she was a complete failure. She felt weariness in her aching bones and tears began to stream down her face as she sat with her sadness, conquered by the weight of her failures, and listening as the buzzer called students back to class.

~

"Well, look who has decided to grace us with her presence this fine day, our resident scholar," Ms. Crandle said loudly to the class in her usual sarcastic tone.

"Bite me!" Rebecca said loud enough to draw some laughter from those seated near by, but not loud enough for her teacher to hear. Her classmates had come to expect polite, carefully measured responses from Rebecca, so her pleasantly surprising harshness brought a good deal more laughter than if it had come from someone a little grungier. "Excuse me, did you say something, Rebecca?" replied Ms. Crandle in a tone that demanded a response.

"I said it's good to be here, Ms. Crandle," replied Rebecca in a tired but even voice as she slid into her seat.

"Yes, I'm sure you did. Why don't you start us off then, Rebecca with a brief reflection on the readings?" As strange as it may sound, Rebecca had never missed a homework assignment. Winning the award for the highest grade point average in her class meant that she had to work harder than about three hundred other students in her grade, some of whom were capable of doing as well, or even better than her. Although Ms. Crandle seemed to enjoy embarrassing students who didn't do the assigned readings, she'd never had that privilege with the star pupil.

The class was amused and a little shocked with Rebecca's response, "I wasn't able to get the reading done. I had a family emergency."

"Oh, I see," said Ms. Crandle in a sensitive voice with a mock look of compassion on her face. "Well, it seems you had a family emergency without your family." The class laughed nervously as they watched Ms. Crandle circling her desk like a hawk, zeroing in on a lonely, unsuspecting field mouse. Many of them had suffered from her ability to humiliate, but Rebecca had always managed to steer clear.

"What do you mean?" asked Rebecca politely.

"Well, I had a lovely conversation with your parents at the banquet last night but, do you know, they didn't have any idea where you were. As a matter of fact, you didn't even show up to receive your award, now did you? Seeing as you're fairly new to making excuses related to homework, might I suggest that in the future, you either include your family in your family crises, or choose a less creative, more traditional approach. Perhaps, 'my dog ate it'. That's always been one of my personal favorites." A sprinkling of half-hearted laughter rose from the desks, but it wasn't directed at Rebecca. Ms. Crandle stood leaning against her desk, arms folded, a look of satisfaction on her face that she'd driven her point home. She'd always used her power to assault feeble-minded students with her wit and her sharp tongue and it hadn't even crossed her mind that today might be different. Smugly satisfied, she turned to gather some notes from her desk.

Although she'd seen it done on many occasions, Rebecca had never been rude to a teacher. On occasion, when the opportunity presented itself, she might question the accuracy of a comment or the validity of a source, but she was always pleasant and polite. But it had been a difficult twenty-four hours and Rebecca felt pushed to her limit, maxed out on patience, and stretched thin on kindness. She didn't feel she had much left to lose so she mustered up a little politeness and spoke with confidence, "Ms. Crandle, am I to understand that you are calling me a liar?" The teacher turned to see Rebecca standing beside her desk, arms folded across her chest, face stern and serious.

"Yes, that is correct. Did you come up with that yourself or did someone whisper it to you?"

Without a moment to check with her brain, Rebecca's mouth had broken loose and was running freely without restraint. "Did your education degree have an entire course in sarcasm and belittling students, or did you pick it up at one of your professional development workshops?" Every head in the class turned at the same time, mouths hanging open, but not a word was spoken as every student stared at their classmate in admiration and amazement.

"Excuse me?" said Ms. Crandle, stepping closer to Rebecca, completely shocked that anyone would dare to confront her. But Rebecca wasn't finished, nor was she afraid. She stepped toward Ms. Crandle her right arm lifted, one rigid finger pointing for emphasis.

"How dare you call me a liar and attempt to humiliate me in front of my friends. You are a cruel person, a terrible teacher, and a spineless bully! You have no right to speak to us the way you do. I've had enough. It's time someone reported your pathetic teaching to the school administration." Rebecca moved to her desk, picked up her back pack and headed for the door. The class simply could not believe what they were seeing, but most of them were having the time of their lives. This action was better than anything they'd see in a movie! "Mr. Edwards is going to know the truth about how you run your classroom," Rebecca said as she passed her teacher, not bothering to look her in the eye as she passed. But Ms. Crandle was not easy to intimidate. She stood like a stone, continuing to mock her student with her sarcastic tone.

"Well done, Rebecca! I'm sure this little outburst will put you in first place for the drama-queen of the year award. When you're having your little visit with our vice- principal, do tell him that you were rude, confrontational, and disruptive in my class. That should help him to decide what to do with you. Now get out!" Her final words smacked of hatred and more than one student felt a chill run down their spine. Rebecca had nothing more to say, she simply walked out leaving the door to the hallway wide open. As Ms. Crandle turned once more to gather her notes and to compose herself, something else was happening in her class. Slowly, students began to rise from their seats in silence, each gathering their backpacks and books and quietly slipping through the open door. They had all had enough. Enough brutality in class. Enough unfair grading. Enough humiliation. It was time to act, and Rebecca's bravery had inspired them to finally take a stand. "Oh, this is beautiful. An entire class mutiny, how original," she said sarcastically, applauding like she'd just watched the final act of a Shakespearean tragedy. But the only tragedy she would witness was the end of her career. In its seventy-five years as a school, MacDonald had never had a full class mutiny. That afternoon, Mr. Edwards met with Rebecca and the entire class of students and he listened carefully. He promised that he would look into the matter and he was a man of his word. Rebecca never heard from that sarcastic teacher again and for the final month of school, she and her classmates smiled every time they saw the substitute teacher sitting at Ms. Crandle's desk.

~

Rebecca had been avoiding the school's back doors all afternoon. She'd taken a different hall to her English class, hoping that she wouldn't have to see the parking lot. She'd even chosen, for the first time, to lock her bike up near the front doors instead of her traditional spot near the small patch of grass out back. It seemed odd that she'd have such a strong aversion to a place that only yesterday morning had been a simple lot. But now this lot had been transformed into the set of a terrifying movie that played itself without permission over and over in her mind. Even her sleep, she'd discovered, would not be a safe place to hide. Rebecca didn't like feeling helpless and she didn't like the idea that a silly parking lot could control her movements around the school.

After her meeting with Mr. Edwards, she wandered into the hall and came face to face with the back doors. Leaning back against the wall, she felt overwhelmed by the sadness of her past twenty-four hours. Rebecca wanted to crawl into a hole and sleep, preferably somewhere far away from people. Her mind wandered to Mason and to the animals at the hospital and she was surprised that she hadn't thought much about them all day, nor did she have any desire to drop in to the hospital after her appointment with the counselor. Right at that moment, Rebecca recognized that she didn't want to care for a single living being: not animal or human. For someone who'd spent her entire life preoccupied with caring for others, this was an odd feeling indeed. Earlier in the day, she'd felt like such a failure but now, as she honestly considered not caring, a presence was slowly creeping under her skin. It was guilt. "How could you not care about Mason?" she said to herself in mild disgust. "Clifton's in a hospital bed in a coma and Amy could be trying to kill herself right now as I lean against this wall." But thoughts are a funny thing. At lunchtime, her thoughts had convinced her that she was terrible at caring, that she should quit. Now she was accusing herself for not caring enough. "Make up your mind girl," she said loud enough to draw a few strange looks from others in the hall. Rebecca dug down deep and found that for the first time in her life she couldn't make herself care, even if she wanted to. Even thinking about Mason and Clifton was not enough to jumpstart her dead battery. It confused her and, for a moment, she felt lost. She bit her lip as she headed out to get her bike for her ride to the counselor's office. "How can I not care? How is that even possible?" she said shaking her head, "I can't just not care! It's who I am."

~ 10 THE CHAIR ~

The black leather recliner seemed out of place in the counselor's office. Rebecca wasn't sure what to expect and she'd certainly never given any thought to the kind of furniture she might find in such a place. She was fairly sure there'd be a couch, 'cause you had to lie down for counseling, or at least she was pretty sure that's how it worked. Riding over on her mountain bike, Rebecca had remembered a story one of her mom's friends had told of her trip to a counselor. She'd claimed she'd been hypnotized. Knocked right out for the whole hour. She couldn't remember anything about her visit, but she said it was worth every penny. She'd told Rebecca that it was kind of like going to a dentist and inhaling sleeping gas before the work began on your teeth. You walk in with a problem and you walk out fixed, it was as simple as that. Like falling off a log. But Rebecca wasn't sure she had a problem that needed fixing and, if she did, she didn't want some stranger messing with her head while she was asleep. The receptionist had let Rebecca into the office and, pleased that there wasn't a couch in the room, Rebecca had chosen a comfy looking black recliner. She'd sat just long enough to notice that the recliner wasn't going to be comfy at all; it was broken and the back was slowly reclining. As she was fiddling with the chair to get the back to stay straight, the office door opened and a middle-aged man stepped into the room carrying a green file folder.

His casual pants and short sleeve shirt made him look like one of the math teachers at MacDonald. She noticed that he had a kind face with a wrinkled forehead that made him look as though he was trying hard to remember something. His stride was unrushed and reminded her of the older man with the stubbly gray hair that often waved at her as she rode to school on her bike. "You must be Becky," he said as he extended his hand. She shook his hand firmly, bristling a little as he butchered her name. Taking a deep breath, she reminded herself that forty five minutes from now her parents would be off her back and her life could get back to normal. "I'm glad I was able to open my schedule on such short notice. My Tuesdays are typically booked up several weeks in advance. For some reason, I seem to have quite a few cancellations this week."

"Yes, thanks for fitting me in. And by the way, I prefer Rebecca." She returned to her seat, immediately wishing she hadn't, as the chair began to recline forcing her to pull herself forward again. The therapist smiled and took his seat across from her. He opened his notes and looked them over carefully. When he was done scanning his pages, he pulled a pen from his shirt pocket and made some quick scribbles on a yellow notepad. "Are you aware that people with the name Rebecca are often referred to as Becky?" he asked in a forced jest.

"Yes, I am, but I do prefer Rebecca," she said returning a pleasant smile.

"I see," he said as he looked at his lap and slowly closed his file. "Your mother mentioned that you might be on edge and I sense some hostility in your voice, don't I?" Rebecca was more than a little surprised by his assumption.

"I'm not on edge and I don't feel hostile," she said. "I just prefer to be called by my full name."

"I see," he said again slowly as he reopened his file and made a few additional notes. "So if you're not on edge or hostile, how do you account for your attack on your mother last night?" The question caught her off guard and suddenly Rebecca felt like her back was against a wall, like she was a terrorist in a holding cell facing an interrogation for her war crimes. She could feel her pulse increasing and she knew that with the kind of day she'd had yesterday, and the horrible dreams she'd had all night, this was probably not the best time for someone to start pushing her buttons.

Straightening her back and using a kind, but factual tone she replied, "I've asked my mom a hundred times not to call me Becky. She doesn't listen. Yesterday was difficult for me. I was overwhelmed and lost my temper. It was a mistake and I made sure my mom knew that I was sorry for the way I treated her."

"As I understand it, you skipped class yesterday and you were involved in an altercation."

"A what?" asked Rebecca.

"Oh, pardon me, that's a pretty big word for someone your age," he said with a condescending chuckle. "I mean, you were involved in a fight."

Rebecca felt like she'd just been slapped. A big word for someone my age, she thought to herself. Is he suggesting that I'm stupid just because I'm a teenager? I wonder if this guy even has a counseling degree?

"Yes," she said evenly, "I was there. I just wanted to see if I could intervene to ameliorate the altercation."

"I see," said the therapist as he paused to rub the back of his neck. "Rebecca, I'm sorry, but I'm not familiar with the word ameliorate."

"Oh, pardon me. That is a pretty big word for someone your age," said Rebecca trying not to smirk. "Let me give you a synonym to make it easier for you to understand." Rebecca paused for effect. "I wanted to see if I could *improve* the situation. Does that help?" she asked with a forced smile.

"I see," he said firmly, opening his note pad again to jot down some observations. Rebecca felt a little bit of remorse for being disrespectful, but she was certainly not interested in being insulted by an arrogant stranger. Although she hadn't been there to receive it, just last night Rebecca had managed to win the award for the highest grade point average in the sophomore class. Last year, she had won the same award as a junior, and she fully expected to win it again next year as a senior. The definition for the word altercation may have slipped her mind but then, with the kind of week she'd had, she was having difficulty remembering simple things.

After the counselor had gathered his thoughts he responded, "So you argue with your mom over little things like your name and you associate with young men who end up in prison for assault. It looks to me like an ongoing pattern of aggression. Do you use drugs?"

As the chair slowly sucked Rebecca backward, she could feel her temper taking on a life of its own. It was an unusual feeling for a young woman proud of her self-control and easy-going personality. She grabbed the arms of the recliner and, with a forceful heave, pulled the back straight with a slam. Her forceful movement at this point in the

71

conversation caught the therapist off guard, giving him the impression that she was aggressive and hostile. "It's not a little thing," she said in a frustrated voice. "Can't you afford to buy a proper chair for people to sit it? This thing is making me crazy."

"Excuse me," said the counselor, not having a clue what she was talking about and completely ignoring her comment about the chair. "What's not a little thing?"

"My name. It's not a little thing. It's who I am. Everyone else calls me Rebecca, even my dad. It's how I want to be known. It's just a matter of respect," she said matter of factly. "It's not something that I want to come between my mom and me. We agreed that she would make the change some time ago."

"And fighting with your mom, how exactly is that respecting her?" he said, smirking like he'd caught a small child in a lie.

"Look, I didn't come here to fight about my name. If this is all there is to counseling, maybe I should go. Is there anything else we need to talk about?"

"I notice that you didn't answer my question about drugs, so let me ask you again. Are you using drugs?"

"No," Rebecca said folding her arms across her chest and making the mistake of leaning back with some force. The chair began to recline again and, as it did, she felt small and frustrated that she couldn't even control a stupid chair. Her anger flared. Why did it feel like everything in her life was spinning out of control? Why was she so irritated by the smallest things? Why couldn't she seem to remember things that were usually important to her? It just felt like she was walking around in a dream.

"Do you drink heavily?" he said without missing a beat.

"What? I'm sorry, what did you say? I'm having some difficulty staying focused today" she said, wrestling again with the chair.

"I said, do – you – drink alcohol?"

"No, I don't drink alcohol. Is that important? When exactly do we get to the counseling part?"

"I see," the counselor said, once again ignoring her question. This time he sat up straight and looked at the ceiling while he tapped his pencil on his top lip, like he was remembering something he'd read in a counseling manual. "So, to sum up, what we have then is a teenager who doesn't do drugs or drink at all. Is that what you're telling me?"

he replied in a tone dripping with sarcasm and disbelief.

"Yes, that's correct," Rebecca said as she looked at her watch.

He smirked, grunted like he'd just been told a joke and began to write on his note pad again. After a long pause he blurted out, "Why don't you tell me about your menstruation cycle?" Rebecca sat for a moment, frozen to her seat in disbelief. No man had ever asked her about her period, not even her dad. She'd watched Zach beaten by his own brother. She'd listened helplessly as Amy had promised to kill herself. She'd sat with Alisa, listening to her speak of her baby and, in the same hour, they'd shared the horrible news that Clifton was in a coma and would never walk again. These were her friends' lives, each one valuable and personal to her. Yesterday had been a day more painful than anything she could have imagined. But Rebecca had been strong through it all. To add to her stress, she knew that a pile of homework waited in her bedroom, eager to receive her focused attention. This is a complete waste of time, she thought to herself. A mental health check-up. Forty-five minutes, in and out, wasn't that what her dad had said this morning?

After yet another deep breath, Rebecca replied with some snap in her voice, "My what?"

"Your period, are you having your period? Sometimes the onset of menstruation, especially for a teenage girl, such as yourself, can elicit a certain sense of disequilibrium and irrational behaviour."

Rebecca straightened her chair, tightened her lips, and leaned forward for effect. "Irrational behavior?" she questioned him softly and slowly as though she wasn't quite sure she'd heard him correctly. Deep inside of her, the hounds of anger were finally being loosed from their barbed-wire kennel, as Rebecca repeated the phrase with considerably more bravado, "Irrational behavior!" As the words slipped across her gritted teeth, she isolated each for emphasis. "Are you out of your mind?" she paused slightly for effect. "Did you get your degree from a mail-order school in Vegas? Listen up mister. I'm not a drug user. I'm not an alcoholic. I'm not having my period. And I'm . . . not . . . irrational!" She spoke these final words with enough intensity that had someone walked into the office at that moment, they would have wondered about the perfect contradiction of words, tone, and facial expression. "One of my closest friends told me that his father gets drunk and then beats him. That friend was beaten up by three guys yesterday and now he's in jail.

One of my closest friends wants to kill herself and she'd rather I keep it a secret so she can go through with it. One of my friends is pregnant but just found out that the father of her baby is now a quadriplegic in a coma. That all happened yesterday. I was overwhelmed; I yelled at my mom. That's all there is to it! Now if this counseling session is over, I have homework that needs to be done."

The counselor hadn't moved. He just watched her, hands folded across the file that lay on his stomach, eyes peering at her, searching for who-knows-what. He took a deep breath and began speaking in a fatherly tone. "I see," he said again slowly. Rebecca thought to herself, if this guy says 'I see' just one more time I am going to lose my mind.

"Becky," he said, suddenly remembering that she'd asked him not to call her that. "Excuse me," he said with a smirk that told her he'd play her little-girl name game. "I mean, Rebecca. Let me tell you something. Sometimes the teen years can seem overwhelming. I know, I was a teenager just like you and I'm pretty sure I know how you're feeling right now. You may find it surprising to know this, but I had problems when I was your age too. I remember the year I turned sixteen, my best friend Ben and I were always fighting." The counselor leaned forward for the first time, laughing a little to himself and moving his hands in the air like sometimes happens when someone is going to tell a story. His file fell to the floor, but he paid no attention. "This one time, oh it has to be thirty years now. No, no, I think it was thirty-four years. Thirty-four?" he chuckled softly. "Where does time go? Anyway, we were on our way to a movie, no, wait. No, I think we were going to the mall. No, my mistake, it was a movie, yes, it was a movie. So we're on our way to this movie and then .. . ."

The counselor never saw it coming. Rebecca had listened to about all she could take. She had just laid her heart bare before this stranger and he hadn't heard a word she'd said. All she could think of was the pain her friends were suffering. Would Clifton ever wake up from his coma? Was Zach in jail? If so, how long would he have to stay there? What if Clifton died? Would Zach be charged for murder? What was Zach's dad going to do to him? How was she going to keep Amy's secret? What if she told someone, would Amy kill herself? Amy could die if Rebecca keeps her secret, but she could die if she doesn't keep the secret. It was just too much. And what about Alisa? What would she decide about her baby? Her head began to swim and she could feel a rapid increase in her breathing. It was just like last night, the same panic overtaking her, controlling her, stifling her thoughts and tying her hands. The air in the room felt thin, like an underwater dive-tank that was running out of oxygen. She could see the counselor's lips moving, but as hard as she tried, she couldn't hear a word he was saying. It was that hollow, off-in-the-distance voice she'd heard last night, just before she'd blacked out. She reached up to rub her face and felt the tingle in her fingers. It was like she was landing after a long parachute free fall. Her feet touched the ground, she could breathe again, she could hear the counselor babbling on about his teen years and suddenly, she snapped. Rebecca bolted from her chair and with her hands balled up into white-knuckled fists, she cried out in frustration, "I don't care about your stupid teen years and I don't care about your friend Ben. And you don't know how I feel. You don't know anything about me. You don't know what I've been through and you haven't heard a bloody word I've said. I'm exhausted and frustrated and sad and afraid and nothing makes sense. I'm here to make my parents happy and my only goal is to get this forty-five minutes of hell over with so I can get on with my life!" Then, feeling a wave of emotional exhaustion, she gently sat down, pressed her face into the palms of her hands and made that sound of frustration that every teenage girl seems to have mastered. The therapist didn't even blink but he did make a kind of grunt-like acknowledgement that sounded to Rebecca like he was surprised that she didn't want to hear his story.

"I see," he said as he picked up his file and noted something on his pad of paper. "Well then, does that feel better?" he asked her.

"Does what feel better?"

"Getting angry, did that help you release some tension?"

"Yes, I guess it did. I'm sorry, I'm not usually like this, it's just that I have a lot on my mind."

"Well, your forty-five minutes of hell, as you called it, are just about up. Before we end our time here together, I'd like to ask you a question if that's OK with you."

"Yes, that's fine," she said a little sheepishly as she began to wonder how the next phone conversation between her mother and this counselor might go.

"Rebecca, have you ever heard of O.D.D.?"

"No, she replied, sitting now on the front edge of her chair to try to keep it from slipping backward again. "What's that?"

"O.D.D. stands for Oppositional Defiance Disorder. I know this may not be easy for you to hear right now, but after what I've seen here today, I'd have to say that you could be the poster girl for this disorder. As the name suggests, it has to do with opposition and defiance, both of which you seem to display quite readily. I'm going to suggest that you talk to your family doctor, or better yet, that you contact a psychiatrist friend of mine for further evaluation."

"Further evaluation!" she said, beginning to panic. "I can't go for further evaluation." She couldn't believe what she was hearing. Her mind was racing, quickly calculating the hours she might have to spend sitting in other offices just like this one. "There must be some other way we can do this."

"I'm afraid not Rebecca. I'll have my secretary provide you with a few contact numbers on your way out. Rebecca, things are difficult for you right now, but with proper treatment and perhaps medication, you'll be able to function like other normal teens."

Other normal teens, she thought to herself. What does he mean other normal teens? I'm a normal teen. There's nothing abnormal about me!

But he was already standing, and extending his hand toward her, "Thank you for coming in. I know this kind of work can be difficult; I admire your strength." And with that he excused himself and left her standing baffled and alone in his office.

The receptionist was on the phone, so Rebecca was able to make her way past without picking up the number for the psychiatrist. As she rode home, she played the session over in her mind. Why had she felt so out of control last night with her mom and now again here with the counselor? She'd never acted like this before. Never had she responded with such disregard for people's feelings. It was all so out of character, like someone else was living in her skin. Just like last night, she felt again the sting of remorse. And what was with her sitting in his office and not being able to hear him speak? It was like she was above them watching them talk, far from her body, but still somehow connected. She wasn't sure what to make of it but she knew one person who would. The most brilliant and caring person she knew. She smirked to herself as she mulled the idea over in her head. She'd see a doctor alright, but she would need more than a psychiatrist to figure this out. This was a job for a veterinarian and she knew right where to find one.

PART III

CHANGE

~ 11 Homework ~

As the rains lightly tapped on her window, Rebecca reached for the off switch on her alarm clock. It was 5:30. "What sort of person would choose to wake up at 5:30 in the morning when they could sleep until 8?" she said, longing for just ten more minutes of sleep. Throwing back the covers, her shoulders protested with knotted, rigid pain. She felt like she'd been through an eight-hour soccer practice. "So much for feeling refreshed," she said, as she forced herself to sit up straight on the edge of the bed. Her toes landed in something wet and sticky. She looked down slowly, knowing exactly what she would see. During the night, Dexter had enjoyed sucking and gnawing on one of her favorite slippers. It was soaked in dog drool and left as a conquered foe by the side of her bed. "Dexter!" she said in disgust, picking up what had once been her slipper. No wonder he hadn't come to wake her: Dexter was in his hiding place. *He's as bad as a two year-old,* she thought to herself as she carried her slipper to the den. Her dog had a very strange habit and no one could figure out how it had developed. Every time Dexter found himself in trouble, or afraid that he might be in trouble, he would squeeze himself into the long narrow space between the back of the couch and the wall. He refused to come when he was called. Not for a biscuit, not for a toy, not even for a walk.

Rebecca grabbed the arm of the couch and slowly pulled it away from the wall. Guilty, remorseful, chocolate-brown eyes, drooping with sadness and a tinge of fear, stared up at her. Convicted by her eyes and the sight of the slipper in her hand, Dexter rolled slowly to one side, shivering and lifting his paw in surrender. His tongue slowly licked his teeth and he tried, with some difficulty, to avoid her eyes.

"Did you do this to my slipper?" she asked with a stern face. It was clear in that moment, as it had been many times before, that even if they could, dogs should never be allowed to play poker or engage in any activity that would require the ability to conceal their feelings. His eyes were his confession and his raised paw and quivering fur told her that he was indeed guilty as charged. Rebecca smiled, "You make me crazy sometimes," she said in a kind voice. "But I guess I owe you a little mercy. You were pretty quick to forgive me the other day when I left you in the house all day. Come on, I'll let you outside."

Hearing the word 'outside', Dexter jumped to his feet and raced through the den and into the kitchen at high speed. But with his legs moving faster than his brain, he missed his turn to the mud room and slid face first on the slick linoleum tile right into the kitchen wall. It looked like something you might see on one of those funniest home-video shows on television. Rebecca laughed so hard that her sides began to hurt and the healing sound of her own joy surprised her. How long had it been since she found pleasure in something simple? Although little more than a day, it seemed like forever. But her dog had a way of helping her get perspective, to refocus and prioritize. As her laughter came to an end, she sat down beside him rubbing his ears and studying his kind face. "Your priorities are simple, aren't they boy?" she said as she held his gaze. "Let me see. If you could talk I think you'd say: spend time with the people you love, run and play, take naps in the sunshine, eat well, be quick to forgive, and every once in a while take a risk, even if it means you might have to hide behind the couch." Rubbing his ears, she smiled again. She didn't cry, but her eyes were open to the idea. She pulled him close for a moment. "Thanks Dexter," she said, "that helps a lot." Rebecca stood and clapped her hands. "Alright, enough of this. Is it time to go outside?" And immediately Dexter's face brightened and he was on his feet, jumping and dancing for joy and leading his favorite girl to the back door.

～

Having finished the mopping, Rebecca was cleaning out the wash bucket when she heard the latch on the front door of the veterinary hospital being unlocked. "That's weird," she said to Mason as he stared at her through the tiny metal bars. "There's not supposed to be anyone here until 8." Walking to the main hall, she spotted Dr. Kristen Anderson struggling to get through the door. She had her keys in her teeth, was balancing a cardboard box on one knee, and with her free hand was attempting to pull the heavy door toward her. Seeing a need, Rebecca ran to help.

"Thanks Rebecca, you're a real life saver. I'm glad I got here before you left." "Why, what's up?" Rebecca said, taking the box and following the doctor down the hall toward the welcoming committee of yelps and barks.

"Good morning everyone," the doctor called. "Isn't it nice to be loved," she said in a loud voice over her shoulder. Unlatching Mason's cage, Dr. Anderson called the old dog to come and took a few moments to speak kindly to him and to rub his wise, gentle face. "Rebecca, Mason's owner was here yesterday."

"That's great," Rebecca said. "When will she be taking him home?"

"Well, that's what we were talking about. Rebecca, Mason is very sick. He's not going to go home and his owner would like us to help him die with dignity. I know how much you care about him, so I thought you might consider assisting me." Rebecca didn't know what to consider first: Mason's death, stopping his suffering, or assisting Dr. Anderson. To say that it created a collision of emotions within her would be an understatement. She didn't want Mason to suffer, but she didn't want to watch him die. This was the first time in two years that Rebecca had been asked to take part in this kind of a procedure. The staff had been reluctant to give the young volunteer a close up of one of the hardest parts of their work. The hardest were cases of animal cruelty, but this wasn't easy either, even though they knew that the service they provided was an act of kindness for their patients and for the people who loved them. Rebecca had remembered seeing some of the staff sitting with people, holding hands, handing out kleenex, and listening to stories. Sometimes after an animal was put down, the office environment would feel heavy as the staff worked through their own feelings of sadness and loss. If the emotional drain got too much to handle, staff were encouraged to take a sick day, just to clear their heads.

Staring at Mason and preparing herself for what was about to happen, Rebecca's mind wandered back to an afternoon not too long ago. She had been cleaning the cages at the hospital and could hear deep sobs coming from an examination room. She'd found out later from Dr. Anderson that the crying woman had been saying goodbye to her son's cat. Her son had been killed in a car wreck a few months previously. The animal was terribly ill and had to be euthanized, but putting her son's pet down had brought a surprising flood of sadness. She wept over the cat, but agonized over the loss of her son, the one grief triggering the other and the two events somehow becoming inseparable in her mind. Wanting Rebecca to understand what she was getting herself into, a few of the vet assistants had explained how putting an animal down could really mess with your head, the images sticking with you day and night, with no respect for the separation between work and home.

Grief is a strange thing, Rebecca thought as she watched Dr. Anderson make the necessary preparations. Looking down at Mason's adoring eyes, she bit her lip hard, forcing herself not to cry. Dr. Anderson was strong, brilliant, and precise. Rebecca did not want to appear weak or incompetent. She cared about Mason, but this was an opportunity to learn about veterinary science. "I'd be honoured to assist you," she finally blurted out, like she'd just been asked out by the man of her dreams. She blushed a little when she heard how silly her reply had sounded.

Dr. Anderson looked into Rebecca's eyes for a moment and then at the ground. "It is no honour to take a life," she said. Rebecca was shocked to notice tiny pools of tears swelling in the corners of the doctor's strong, wise eyes. "But as a healer Rebecca, you have an obligation to admit to the broken and to yourself when there is simply nothing more that you can do. You will never make it as a vet if you think that by your efforts you can heal them all." Dr. Anderson touched Mason on the head again and this time bent down to check his pulse.

"Will we wait for the owner?" Rebecca asked.

"No. She's elderly and has recently lost her husband. It's not uncommon for people to say goodbye and to leave the actual procedure to us. She said her goodbyes yesterday and she's asked me to call her once Mason is gone." They walked Mason down the hall to an examination room and closed the door and Dr. Anderson looked again at Rebecca. "Why don't you hold his head on your lap and pet him. A few moments after I make the injection he'll stop breathing, but you should know that his eyes may stay open." She stroked his face and spoke kindly to him as Rebecca stared into the deep brown eyes that said, 'I trust you with my life'. And for a moment she felt the sting of betrayal. How can you do this to him? He trusts you! cried an accusing voice in her mind. A rush of panic ran through her veins. Do something! Save him! Everything in her wanted to grab the needle from Dr. Anderson's hand and throw it across the room, but instead she stroked Mason's fur and watched as her animal friend took his last breath, with his head resting on her lap.

It was the first time that Rebecca had seen death up close. People spoke of it like it was something to be avoided at all costs, but somehow this moment seemed sacred to her. Not something terrible and awkward, but natural and strangely peaceful. She wondered if Clifton might die like Mason, drifting off to sleep with his head on Alisa's lap, pressed against her tummy and their baby. People are so difficult to understand, Rebecca thought, as sadness began to set up camp in her heart. Clifton was fighting to stay alive and Amy was fighting to die. How much sense did that make? Rebecca looked up at Dr. Anderson, who by now had set the syringe back on its tray and had taken some tissue from her pocket, one for each of them. "I know it sounds funny," Rebecca heard herself saying, "but I didn't think something like this would ever make you cry." Dr. Anderson wiped a cheek dry and gave a little chuckle. "Sometimes caring too much can be the worst kind of gift."

Rebecca sat quietly considering the statement, one she'd most certainly have rejected under different circumstances. "You mean caring is bad?" she said as she tried to understand what Dr. Anderson was telling her.

"No, caring is a good thing. Are you familiar with the word empathy?"

"Doesn't it mean that you can feel other people's pain?"

"That's right. It's sometimes described as the ability to walk in someone else's shoes. But think about that for a moment. Walking around in one person's shoes might be manageable, but we see hundreds of people in this office every month. And most of them are suffering because their pet is in pain." Rebecca was having some difficulty understanding. Dr. Anderson continued, "You see, the ability to empathize, or to care deeply for others, is like a thick rubber band.

It can stand up to almost any single job, but if you stretch the rubber band over and over and over again, what happens to it?"

"It doesn't work anymore," said Rebecca.

"Exactly, it's like the elastic is too tired to do its job. Empathy is just like that elastic. Our desire to care is pretty strong, but some days our caring is stretched to the limits. Have you ever had a day like that Rebecca? When you felt your caring was stretched to the limits?" The question caught her off guard and Rebecca's eyes began to well up with tears, feeling as full as a water bomber on its way to a fire. "Veterinarians take a series of classes just to learn how to recognize and manage what one of my professors used to call 'compassion fatigue'."

Her bottom lip was quivering as Rebecca sadly spoke the words, "compassion fatigue." Her eyes released the water in a flood and Rebecca found herself once again overwhelmed, but this time it had nothing to do with Mason or her friends. She was terrified by the idea that too much caring could actually damage her ability to empathize. What would her life be like if she lost her ability to care? The idea had never even crossed her mind and just the thought of it was too much for her to bear.

"Rebecca, what is it? Your tears don't seem to be about Mason anymore."

"Do you mean that if my empathy gets stretched too much, I could actually lose my ability to care about my friends or my family?"

"Yes, that's exactly what I'm saying. But it's difficult to recognize and the symptoms don't typically make sense unless you understand how compassion fatigue works. I suspect that counselors with no knowledge of the problem are coming up with all kinds of wild ideas." Rebecca paused, remembering that the counselor had told her only yesterday that she was the poster-child for Oppositional Defiance Disorder. If Dr. Anderson was right, this could be an example of a counselor being completely wrong. "It's a good idea to limit our caring, just so we don't stretch ourselves too much."

"Limit my caring!" Rebecca said forcefully. "How can I limit my caring? My friends need me," she said, as again her crying began to intensify. "I can't just stop caring. I can't stop!" she said as she wept with both of her hands now pressed to her face. "I can't stop. My friends need me and . . ." but her crying had gained momentum and Rebecca was bordering on hysterics. She could feel herself loosing control of her breathing again and the room began to tilt and fade. "No, not again," she said out loud in a firm voice. "Not again," she panted, not able to slow down or to think straight, listening as the pounding of her own heart exploded in her head.

Taking control of the situation like a trained professional, Dr. Anderson spoke in a commanding voice. "Rebecca, I need you to calm down. Listen to me. I need you to breathe with me now, slowly." Rebecca felt dizzy and the voice in the room took on a hollow distant sound. She was certain that she'd been talking with someone only moments ago, but as hard as she tried, she couldn't remember who it was. And then without warning, just as had happened in the counselor's office, she felt herself floating back to the ground, like she was coming to the end of a long parachute jump. She could hear Dr. Anderson somewhere close by and, looking to her left, she saw her on her hands and knees. Why is she on her hands and knees? Rebecca thought, as slowly she began to realize what had happened. She leaned back against the exam room wall and dabbed the sweat beads from her forehead with a tissue. This couldn't keep happening to her; she had to figure out what was wrong.

By the time they left the examination room, a number of the vet assistants had arrived and Dr. Anderson asked if they would take care of the dog's body. Rebecca excused herself and slipped into the restroom to freshen up and compose herself for the general public. As she headed back toward the cages, she found Dr. Anderson waiting for her. "Rebecca, a few months back I asked you to do some research and write a report on lime disease. Do you remember that?" Rebecca nodded her head that she did indeed remember. For most teens her age, it would have been a painful assignment, but she'd loved every minute of it. "You seemed to enjoy that assignment. Would it be alright if I gave you another one?" It seemed an odd time to give her homework, but at least Rebecca felt like Dr. Anderson had a bit of respect left for her. "I got this book at a Humane Society conference in the States back in the fall." She handed her the paperback and Rebecca immediately noticed the picture of the golden lab on the front.

She read the title out loud, "Compassion Fatigue in the Animal-Care Community," and she stared at Dr. Anderson. "You want me to study compassion fatigue?"

"Yes, I do. And I've given you three tasks to research. They're written on the inside of the front cover. I'd also like you to complete the Compassion Satisfaction and Fatigue Test. It will help us to know if this is something that you're currently experiencing and to what degree. Here's the catch: I leave tomorrow afternoon for a conference in Toronto and then I'm taking some vacation time for a week after that. If you'd like to talk about this before I leave, it'll have to be tomorrow morning for breakfast, my treat. Are we on?"

Rebecca smiled, "I think I can clear my calendar for breakfast."

"Good then, it's settled. I'll pick you up at 6:30. Bring the book and make sure you have your completed work in writing."

~ 12 BREAKTHROUGH ~

It felt strange being in class again. It was Wednesday morning and Monday already seemed like another life lived long ago in a parallel universe. Zach had awoken Monday morning to his mother's singing and felt encouraged by her new zest for life. His dad's unexpected visit had rekindled his smoldering hatred and Zach had promised himself that Clifton would pay. And pay he did: for his own stupidity and arrogance. But Zach felt no joy, only regret that his brother would never walk again. And then there was Rebecca. He'd felt like such a fool pouring out his heart, telling her things he'd never told anyone before. But he had to admit, it was a clean feeling, like starting over. She'd listened to him and she'd been the only one in his corner during the fight. He wasn't used to someone sticking up for him and, at the time, it had seemed kind of funny. But to Zach, loyalty was serious business. He would never forget what Rebecca had tried to do and he was eager to find a way to say thanks.

As Zach had sat in his cell, he'd thought about Rebecca. He figured that she'd be upset about the fight and his injuries and he'd wanted to call her to let her know that he was alright, to say thanks, to see if she was OK, and quite frankly just to hear her voice. But free phone service wasn't part of the guest package in the prison, so he'd simply sat with his thoughts. It hadn't occurred to him that Clifton had been hurt all that badly and it wasn't until one of the officers tried to use Clifton's injury to get a full confession, that Zach understood just how bad things were for his brother. Except for the seriousness of Clifton's injury, the whole scene had been normal as far as fights go. Trash talk, punches, kicks, blood, and of course, it was no surprise to Zach that he'd come out on top. The real shock had come when the police had wanted to press charges for drunkenness, public disturbance, assault, even attempted murder. They were open to a variety of possibilities, desperate to charge him with anything that would stick. Monday night, they'd taken his statement and the police had done their best to get him to confess. They'd promised him in caring tones that being honest was the best way of ensuring that things would go smoother in the long run. They wanted the best for him or so they said. Both of the officers present pressed him to admit that he'd come to the parking lot drunk, looking to hurt his brother, and that he'd hit him so hard that Clifton had fallen. They'd also wanted him to admit that he'd assaulted two innocent bystanders in the fight. But Zach wasn't stupid and he was a great deal more honest than anyone was ready to believe.

After a few hours, the police had given up and placed him back in his cell, completely frustrated that he wouldn't change his story. "I hope you like the food around here kid," one officer had joked as he closed the cell door, "'cause you're gonna be eatin it for a long time." Zach spent the night sleeping on a thin green mattress thrown over a board which rested on a poor excuse for a cot that desperately needed a few shots of oil. By late Tuesday afternoon, Officer Preston had managed to figure out what had happened but what she would never clearly understand was why. According to their tests, Zach hadn't been drinking. It hadn't made sense at first, not with him smelling so strongly of alcohol, but after interviewing Rebecca and the other spectators they'd managed to piece it all together, play by play. Zach had been released late last night and, since his mother was at work, he'd walked home alone with Officer Preston's parting words ringing in his head: "If you enjoy your freedom young man, I suggest you consider some lifestyle changes. You keep fighting and eventually your overnighter is going to turn into an extended stay. Sitting in a prison cell is no way to spend your life. I suggest you think long and hard about that."

Back in class, Zach was listening as Mr. Hiebert summarized the previous lesson. "It gets results," the teacher said in a firm loud voice as he flashed the power point response onto the screen. Under the words he'd typed: "quote by Zach McNabb." He was a good teacher and students generally liked him. Often his classes would begin like this, with a brief summary of the previous discussion to help students remember the topic. "Who can tell me what this means and why it's important for our class?" Immediately his classmates turned to stare at Zach, thinking that it was his responsibility to explain the quote. After a moment of awkward silence, Mr. Hiebert also turned his eyes on him. "Well Zachary, could you give us a little refresher?"

Zach took a deep breath. Maybe the cop was right, maybe it was time for a change. Looking up at Mr. Hiebert, he answered the question. "It means violence gets faster results than peace."

"That's correct Zach," the teacher said, stopping to clarify lest he be misunderstood. "That is to say, this phrase used by Mr. McNabb on Monday was intended to mean that violence is a faster, more effective method of achieving the desired results." Mr. Hiebert had been strolling around the front of the class, his right hand on his bearded chin, and his eyes fixed on his shoes. But now he turned to face Zach. "And have you had an opportunity to test your hypothesis, Mr. McNabb? Have you proven this theory that violence is indeed more effective?" Everyone in the class, including the teacher, had heard about the fight and Mr. Hiebert had been briefed in a staff meeting regarding Clifton's condition. The teachers had been told that Zach was not the aggressor, but few of them had been convinced. Mr. Hiebert knew that having this conversation this soon after the fight was indeed risky and he wasn't sure how things were going to turn out.

"Yes, I've tested my theory," Zach said, working hard not to sound as sad as he felt. His response caught the attention of the class and the room grew quiet. "I tested it on my brother," he said, choosing this time not to lift his head. Mr. Hiebert stared at Zach with kindness in his eyes and he sat slowly on the edge of his desk, intrigued by the response.

"And what did you discover, son?"

Zach was caught off guard by the word *son* and, as he looked up into kind eyes, he wondered what his life would have been like had he been born Zach Hiebert. What if this man had tucked him into bed every night and invested in his life everyday? A lump caught in his throat and, for a moment, Zach looked away, feeling suddenly like he was sitting in the middle of the class with no clothes on. He cleared his throat, sat up straight and looked back at Mr. Hiebert, "I discovered that I was right, violence gets fast results." Zach paused for a moment and Mr. Hiebert forced himself not to show any sign of disappointment.

"Oh, I see," the teacher said as he began to move toward his computer.

But Zach wasn't finished. "I also discovered that sometimes I don't like the results I get. It's like you want winning a fight to feel good, to feel right, like you just scored a goal, or got asked out, or got a good mark on something you thought you failed. But the more I fight, the worse it feels. It just feels like . . ." and there Zach paused for a moment. He wasn't used to identifying his emotions and he'd just driven himself up a dead end and right to the end of his words. The class hung on in silence, some were even starting to tear up, knowing what had happened to Clifton. Mr. Hiebert didn't move a muscle; he hardly breathed, sensing that something significant was happening to Zach right before his eyes. This is what it's all about, he thought to himself in anticipation as he watched his most resistant learner breaking through to an entirely new reality.

"I guess it just feels disappointing," he finally said. Some of his classmates stared out the window fighting off the tears, while others simply looked at their desktops. After sitting with his thoughts for a moment, Zach continued, this time stunning everyone, even himself, as he took a giant step toward becoming the man his father would never be. It was only a few words, but they were weighted with decision and life change. Zach had no idea that the words he was about to speak would begin, even that very day, to guide the way he would choose to engage his world for the rest of his life. Perhaps Mr. Hiebert was the only one in the room who understood how powerful Zach's comments were, for as the words fell from Zach's lips, his teacher stood wiping his eyes with his sleeve. "I'm tired of being disappointed," Zach said as he swallowed hard, a little surprised by his own emotion. "It sounds stupid but," he hesitated, like a soldier stepping gingerly onto a mine field. "I think I'd like some peace for a change." And that was all he said.

By the time the buzzer set students free for the day, the rumour mill had taken Zach's need for peace and given it a new spin, shocking everyone who heard: 'Zach McNabb isn't fighting anymore'. But not everyone was buying it and some were eager to find out for themselves, including a football player with a sore shoulder and one with a broken knee.

~ 13 A DOUBLE-EDGED SWORD ~

Dexter was absolutely no help when it came to doing anything that didn't directly involve his personal entertainment. Stroking his soft hair as he lay beside her on the bed, Rebecca's mind wandered to Mason. She felt the numbness of grief, but was so glad that these brown eyes still smiled up at her. Holding the book Dr. Anderson had given her, she thumbed through the first few chapters, casually thinking about a life with no ability to care for her friends. She thought about the school counselor that she and Alisa had visited. It felt good to know that Alisa was going to have a few adults to help her make decisions about her pregnancy. She wondered how Amy was doing and felt a little irritated that both her emails and phone calls were being left unanswered. As for Zach, Rebecca's parents had asked her not to contact him for a few days and, although she hadn't liked the restriction, she'd understood their concern. That explained why Rebecca felt a little sneaky that Wednesday afternoon when she saw the email waiting from Zach. She quickly reasoned that she'd been obedient to her parents. She had not contacted Zach; he had contacted her. Besides, it was just an email. What harm could there be in reading a few lines? In the short note, Zach filled in the gaps explaining what had happened after she'd been taken from the parking lot. After a brief description of the prison accommodations and the questioning, he thanked her for being in his corner at the fight. Reading the final line, Rebecca recognized a little something flutter in her stomach. He wanted to know if they could get together on Friday night, and it made her smile.

Now anyone who's ever done homework knows that the very worst place is the bed. Of course Rebecca knew this and after thinking about her friends, daydreaming, petting her dog, and thinking about Zach's email, she thought it best to stay at her desk. She'd have to take notes as she read, but she couldn't hold the book open and type at the same time. So much for the computer, she thought to herself as she pulled a note pad from her top drawer and opened the book to find Dr. Anderson's first task: "Explain compassion fatigue." That seemed simple enough. As Rebecca flipped to the first chapter, her mind wandered off again like a curious two-year-old in a mall. What had Dr. Anderson said about empathy? Rebecca thought for a moment. "It's like an elastic that's too tired to do its job." But there was something else. What did she say? Suddenly it came to her. "Limit your caring." Those had been the words that had sent Rebecca into a downward tailspin. What a weird thing for a doctor to say, she thought but, in the next few moments, she would begin to understand.

The first thing that struck her was an odd phrase about empathy. Even though it wasn't part of the assignment, Rebecca decided to write it down to talk about tomorrow at breakfast. "Empathy is a double-edged sword." Maybe that's what Dr. Anderson was talking about. Empathy is good for the patient but not always so good for the helper. Reading further, she found a section that made her feel as though someone had been following her around for the past two days taking notes. It was a list of normal emotional reactions a person might have when working with people who are suffering. As she began to read the list, her voice quickly sank to a whispered hush. It was like she was reading from an ancient holy book. As the words hit the air, Rebecca felt a strange mix of shock and relief. "Those suffering with compassion fatigue might feel: powerless, helpless, ineffective, anxious, afraid, terrified, guilty, full of rage, numb, shutdown, exhausted, sad, hypersensitive, like they're riding on an emotional roller coaster, overwhelmed, and severely weakened." She read the list again, this time with a smile working its way onto her face. "Well, I guess I'm normal Dex," she said with a shake of her head.

Putting the book down on the desk, Rebecca picked up her pen and looked again at the assignment. This list seemed to fit in with the second task. She read Dr. Anderson's second task, "Look carefully at the chart on page 23 and describe the risks associated with caring." These seemed to be risks too, so Rebecca added this list to her second section and then quickly flipped over to page 23. She saw the list that Dr.

Anderson had wanted her to study, but her eyes also fell on something she hadn't expected. On page 22, the author had written, "Secondary trauma survivors (caregivers) try to help primary trauma survivors (victims) with empathy and compassion and frequently experience symptoms similar to those of the victims. This is secondary trauma." Rebecca wrote this down and began to think it over. "If this is true," she thought out loud, "then a caregiver might feel the very same things as a victim. But that can't be right. How could I ever feel what Zach felt? My dad has never been a drunk or hit me with a belt." A flash of white-hot memory exploded in Rebecca's mind and, for the first time since Monday night, she was able to remember what happened just before she passed out. Both of her hands went to her mouth at the same time as Rebecca gasped, feeling the full weight of the memory wash over her. It was the belt. My dad's belt. That sound, just like Zach's memory of his dad taking off his belt. But how? She looked again at what she'd written down, "The caregiver can experience the same kinds of things as the victim." But how can that happen? This was something she and Dr. Anderson would definitely need to talk about.

Returning to the book, Rebecca was beginning to feel her hunger for knowledge kicking in. She loved research. Noticing that there was a list of symptoms a caregiver might have when experiencing secondary traumatic stress, Rebecca picked up her pen again and began to write: "intrusive thoughts, nightmares, flashbacks, feelings of detachment, avoiding activities that remind one of the event, sleep disturbance, hypervigilance, and fatigue." She looked at the list and thought about her life since Monday night. "Intrusive thoughts," she said tapping her pen against the desk lightly. "That makes sense. I can't seem to control when images of Zach, or Amy, or Clifton walk right into my mind. Maybe that's what that means." She made a few notes and looked at the next word on the list. Nightmares. That's an easy one to check off, she thought, and flashbacks, they're kind of like intrusive thoughts. Detachment was harder for Rebecca to see and it took her a few moments of thinking and talking it over with Dexter before the lights started to come on. Maybe that's why it's been so hard to connect with people like Shae. Listening to Amy was hard too and, by the time I got to Alisa, I was totally out of it. When it came to avoiding activities Rebecca paused, thinking this one hadn't really been an issue. That is, unless she counted her fear of the parking lot. I've been avoiding the parking lot because it reminds me of the fight. And I sure didn't want to go to the vet hospital after school. Sleep disturbance and fatigue were no-brainers, but Rebecca didn't recognize the word hypervigilance. She knew what vigilance meant, but she thought she'd check her dictionary just in case Dr. Anderson quizzed her. The definition read: "Hypervigilance: an intensified state of paying attention, severely limiting a person's ability to focus on specific tasks or engage in reflective thinking. Attention is constantly focused on scanning for threatening stimuli; increased state of guardedness or watchfulness, may be a sign of escalating anxiety or agitation." Rebecca was intrigued by the definition and was glad that she'd looked it up, but she recognized that she hadn't been constantly looking over her shoulder for threats. "Hypervigilance, sounds more like Zach's life than mine," she said to herself. And then she chuckled a little, "At least there's one symptom on the list that I don't have. That's encouraging!"

As Rebecca studied the chart carefully, her eyes came to rest on the words *loss of purpose*. Her own haunting words began to echo in her mind, "If my caring only hurts others, then I guess it's time to stop caring." For the first time in her life, Rebecca had come to the end of her ability to care; she had thought she was losing her mind. But right here on this chart it said that part of the cost of caring for others was losing sight of purpose, losing sight of the love for caring. Rebecca was only beginning to learn that research, even good research, often left a student with as many questions as answers. She kind of understood how caring could lead to a loss of purpose, but it was something she and Dr. Anderson would need to explore together.

Finally, with sadness touching the edges of her lips, Rebecca saw the one symptom on the list that stabbed deeply at her heart: anger. In her anger she had acted like a spoiled brat but now she understood why. Although they had been angry with each other before, she had never treated her mom as poorly as she had in their spat about her name. Rebecca felt bad and she wanted to do something to make it up to her mom. She jotted a note in the margin: buy flowers for mom. She smiled as she thought about how much her mom had meant to her over the years. As her mind began to wander, she thought about a few other things she might do over the next few days, just to make sure her mom knew she was loved. There were other things in the book that made a lot of sense but Rebecca had done enough research for now.

As she reached over and scratched Dexter behind his ear with her left hand, her right hand turned to the compassion fatigue test located in the back of the book. "I guess it's time to get this test done, Dex," she said, winking at her barely conscious companion. "This should be a breeze for an honor student!" But this would be the one time in her life when intelligence would not help her to conquer a test. Rebecca's wish would come true though; she would get a very high score on this little exam. Of course, she had no way of knowing that the higher the score, the bigger the problem might be. But her meeting with the good doctor was about to make things painfully clear.

~ 14 REMEMBER MASON ~

"67!" Rebecca said in frustration as she picked at her breakfast. "I've never failed a test before! This isn't some random trigonometry quiz; this really matters to me. What am I supposed to do now, stop caring?"

Dr. Anderson was smiling kindly and nodding her head as she sipped her herbal tea. "I know you're discouraged, but the nice thing is, you can't fail this test. The score means your caregiving might be hurting you, that's all. It's not a clinical diagnosis; it's just food-for-thought. What do you think I scored the first time I answered those sixty-six questions on the Compassion Fatigue Test?" Rebecca hadn't given it much thought but it made sense that Dr. Anderson had taken the test.

"I don't know," she said, still pouting over her results.

"I got an 81."

"Wow, that's terrible!" said Rebecca feeling good that she'd done better than the doctor but not feeling so good that she'd just told her that her score was terrible. "Oh, I'm sorry," said Rebecca, quickly recovering.

But Dr. Anderson was laughing, "It's not a problem, you're right. If 31-35 is moderate risk and 41 is extremely high risk for compassion fatigue, then I'd say it's pretty safe to conclude that 81 is a really bad score." She was shaking her head in disgust. "But what do we learn when we see scores like 67 and 81? What does it mean for us and for our caregiving?" They both paused for a moment to think.

"I did my homework, but I guess I'm still not sure," said Rebecca as she traced an invisible number 67 in the air with her fork.

"Let's back up a little and look at your homework. Before we can understand the numbers we scored, we have to know what the label compassion fatigue means. Do you have your notes?"

Rebecca reached into her backpack and brought out her pad of paper. She flipped to the right spot and began to read, "Compassion stress is the demand to be compassionate and effective in helping. Animal-care professionals experience compassion fatigue when they are traumatized by trying to help. Compassion fatigue is exhaustion due to compassion stress, the demands of being empathic, and helpful to those who are suffering." Looking up, she watched as the doctor gathered her thoughts.

"Is it fair to say then, that we both felt compassion stress when we wanted to help Mason?" Rebecca nodded in agreement and the doctor continued. "Compassion fatigue is the result of compassion stress. It's like the empathy elastic we talked about. Too much stretching and things stop working properly. The real key here is to pay attention to the *compassion stress*, or *secondary traumatic stress* as it's sometimes called." Dr. Anderson reached across the table and picked up the book. "Rebecca, with your score of 67, I wonder if the loss of Mason is only one of the difficult things in your life right now. Am I right?"

Rebecca smiled as her mentor's eyes held onto hers in support. "That's kind of an understatement," she said quietly.

"Well, we've got some time and I've got a fresh pot of tea, so why don't you bring me up to speed?"

Rebecca felt the tears rush to her eyes and the suddenness of the moisture on her face had her reaching for her napkin, even before she'd said anything. "I'm sorry," she managed to blurt out. But Dr. Anderson wasn't interested in apologies. She just wanted to give this young, promising woman an opportunity to feel the kind of support that she'd no doubt been providing for everyone else but herself.

Sitting back in her orange bench seat, Rebecca sighed a little, wondering if this was how Zach had felt after he'd dumped his garbage. "That's some week," the doctor finally said with a smile. "It's amazing that your score isn't 167!" They both laughed and enjoyed the bond that a bit of compassion can create. "You know, this test has another score that you might find interesting. It doesn't just measure your risk level for compassion fatigue; it also provides a compassion satisfaction measure."

"I remember seeing that," said Rebecca. "It was one of the things I wanted to talk with you about." The doctor went on to explain how the compassion satisfaction score was an indication of how much you love caring. She told Rebecca that the higher the score in this category, the faster she's likely to rebound from the effects of secondary traumatic stress.

"My score for compassion satisfaction was 101, that's good, right?""Yes, it's great! It means you love caring for animals and people and that you feel a great deal of satisfaction from your caring, even though at times you might find it emotionally challenging. If this number is low and your compassion fatigue number is high, you probably want to look for a different kind of work. But your numbers come out a lot like my own once did."

Dr. Anderson's words jumped out at Rebecca and immediately she found herself leaning forward, eager to know more. "What do you mean, 'once did'?" she asked in a determined voice.

A look of surprise spread across the doctor's face. "I'm sorry Rebecca," she said, "You don't know, do you? I mean, how could you?" she said smiling. Leaning forward with a twinkle in her eye she said, "Rebecca you're not stuck with these compassion fatigue numbers for life. You can change them!"

The young scholar felt like she was back in grade one learning to write her name. "What do you mean? The numbers can change? Do you mean I can get a better score? This is great! What's the best score to get? How can I do it?" She reached across the table and picked up the book from beside the doctor's plate and turned to the right page in the back. "30, that's low risk. I want my score to be 30."

"Well before we do that, why don't we talk about the second assignment I gave you? Do you have it there?"

"Yes," said Rebecca, feeling a little proud that she'd finished her homework. She turned the pages of her note pad and found where she'd copied the assignment from the book: 'Look carefully at the chart on page 23 and describe the risks associated with caring.' The chart in the book was called the Personal Impact of Secondary Traumatic Stress and it listed a number of things a caregiver might experience after working with people in pain. Rebecca liked the way it had been designed with sections showing how secondary traumatic stress could affect a helper's thinking, emotions, behaviour, spirituality, relationships, and their body. "I hope you don't mind, but I wasn't really thinking about this stuff from a veterinarian perspective. It's just that, so much of this applies to me right now," Rebecca said, hoping she hadn't disappointed Dr. Anderson.

"Not a problem, Rebecca. Actually with the kind of week you've had, it makes more sense to think in the present. There will be plenty of time to apply your findings to the life of a vet later on. So what did you discover?"

Rebecca took some time to explain all of the symptoms that she'd seen in her own life that week and to note a few that had been absent. She was surprised to discover that she and Dr. Anderson both experienced disorientation and lack of concentration when they were overwhelmed by secondary traumatic stress. "The key to staying healthy is self-understanding. The better you know yourself, the more effective you'll be in caregiving. That's why we have to know what overwhelms us and, when we're feeling overwhelmed, we have to know what to do about it." Dr. Anderson paused and looked hard at her young apprentice across the table, "And it's best to plan your escape route, before your house catches fire!"

Rebecca took a moment to digest these words before speaking. "You mean, plan ahead, right?"

"Exactly! Traumatic stress overwhelms our ability to think clearly so, if you want to stay healthy, you're going to have to create your escape route before you find yourself in the middle of a fire. Make sense?"

As they continued to look at the list, Rebecca talked about her fierce self-doubt, how she'd blamed herself for Amy's decision, and how she'd felt so helpless. Dr. Anderson assured her that these feelings were normal and she made sure that Rebecca knew that Amy's choices were not her failures. "Making other people's choices your failures is one of the fastest ways to compassion fatigue and to a nervous breakdown. Believe me: been there, done that."

In addition to listening to Rebecca's concerns, Dr. Anderson wanted to create an action plan for exposing Amy's secret as soon as they were done their breakfast. "One of the best ways to feel overwhelmed is to go it alone, Rebecca. Do it all yourself. Keep all the secrets. Carry all the weight. Put on that red superwoman cape and jump over tall buildings, catch bullets in your teeth, save the world! It's called the superhero syndrome and it's the fastest way to make yourself sick, angry, miserable, and ineffective." Although Dr. Anderson's description of the superwoman had made Rebecca laugh, the truth of it had gripped her by the throat and made her a little angry and even resentful. Had she looked over her shoulder right at that moment, she would have been very surprised not to see a red cape dangling down over the back of the seat. It had been a perfectly uncomfortable description of Rebecca, the superhero.

As she talked about her sense of sadness and irritability and how she'd blown up at her mom, she was struck by something significant. "The part I don't understand is how it changes you so fast," Rebecca said. "I mean, I've never treated my parents as badly as I did this week. I've never talked back to a teacher. I'm not high maintenance. I'm not irritable and moody like some of the girls I know. It's like a few traumatic events have made me a different person."

Dr. Anderson let the words hang in the air for a moment before responding. "Rebecca, you have no idea how wise you are. I'd like you to add what you just said to your notes." Dr. Anderson lowered her eyes for the first time and said very quietly, "Rebecca, caring changes you. There's a cost you need to consider every time you say yes to a friend, or to a patient." Rebecca could feel her frustration beginning to boil and, after a few moments of silence, she brought her balled up fist down on the table with a thud.

"Then why bother?" she said in an angry tone. "I have all these symptoms, and a 67, and nightmares, and sadness, and I have this stupid cape on my back, and it's all going to change me. So why should I care? Why bother?" Rebecca let out a sigh disguised as a grunt and leaned back hard into the seat, her head resting on the top edge so she could stare at the ceiling.

It was a good question and Dr. Anderson could tell that the conversation had exposed a few nerves. Finally, the doctor thought to herself, I didn't think this girl's shell would ever crack. All along she'd wanted her young apprentice to feel the sting of caring. Describing compassion fatigue and looking at the list were the doctor's ways of getting Rebecca to come face to face with the painful realities of caregiving so that she could help her to buy into the idea of self-care. Now that a few nerves had been exposed, perhaps she could help her take the next step. It's time we find out what this girl's really made of, she thought to herself, as she prepared to poke some of the exposed nerves.

Sitting face to face with this young woman, Dr. Anderson recalled a crucial experience from her own journey. She'd always loved animals, and long before she was a doctor, she'd been with animal control. It had been a cold October weekend and the rain was showing signs of turning to snow. A call came in from the local police station asking her to meet a number of officers at a farm just outside of town. The scene was like nothing she could ever have imagined. Numbers of different animals tied to stalls, starved thin, frightened, and diseased. It took days to clean up the tragedy and many of the animals were beyond help. One by one, innocent lives were lost while the owner walked away with a minor criminal charge. Over the next few months, Kristen Anderson, the superwoman, had gone on a 'save the world' rampage. She'd buried herself in her work, refused her friends' attempts to help, wallowed in her rage, and finally made herself very sick. Weak from lack of nutrition and inconsistent sleep, she'd collapsed at work. Knowing that Kristen was stubborn, her boss had put it to her firmly, get help or get a new job. And that was the beginning of her grueling journey back to sanity and to health. She'd had to learn how to leave work at work, how to let go of pain without being crushed by guilt, how to set healthy limits, how to recognize her own human limitations, and most importantly, how to develop a supportive network of people who would care for her when things got difficult. And Kristen had had to learn to live without her red cape. It was the kind of early life training that had made her into a compassionate and healthy veterinarian, but very few had any idea just how difficult the journey had been. How ironic, that years later she would sit across a restaurant table giving a young woman the kind of painful advice that she'd once refused to listen to herself.

"Why bother? Is it worth it? Those are questions only you can answer Rebecca. But as you think about the cost, remember Mason. Caring for the suffering might be costly, but it's also a gift."

Rebecca shifted uncomfortably at the sound of Mason's name and felt a pang of guilt run through her veins. She knew she would do it all again, even if she'd known she would lose him. And she would sit with Zach again, even if she knew what he would say. She would stand in that gravel parking lot terrified, and she would listen to Amy, and she would weep with Alisa. She'd do it all again, even if it meant nightmares and panic attacks and sadness. But then she heard a red cape flapping in the wind behind her and she knew she was stuck. She would do it all again! That was the problem! She would keep caring for others and she would always feel sick. She would never change her score! She might as well get a big red 67 tattooed on her forehead.

"Rebecca. Do you really want to drop your score to 30?"

"Yeah, I do," she said, already convinced that it would never happen. "What do I have to do?"

"Why don't you tell me," Dr. Anderson said. "Don't we have one final homework question to consider?"

Rebecca checked her notes, "Yeah, number three. You asked me to write down three things that I'll need to do to stay healthy?'"

"If you combine your answers with what we've talked about this morning, you'll be well on your way to dropping your score to 30. But you need to understand that once in a while you're going to have a 67 kind of week. Your score might shoot up through the roof, but you don't have to stay there, not if you have a good escape route."

"This question was hard. I don't think I answered it very well. I guess I'm just not sure what I need. I kind of feel stuck. I need to care for my friends, but I need to care for me. I can't just say no to my friends when they need me."

Dr. Anderson smiled. Time to step on another nerve, she thought to herself. "Rebecca, what do you think would happen if you said no to a friend?" Dr. Anderson paused for effect and let the idea simmer in the mind of her young apprentice. It seemed like a clear enough question, but by the look on Rebecca's face, Kristen could see that this was the very first time the idea had ever crossed her mind.

"It just wouldn't be right. You wouldn't turn a suffering animal away would you? How could you expect me to turn a friend away?" Rebecca's cape was snapping in the wind, her muscles were bulging, her hands planted firmly on her hips. But it was time for this teenage superhero to get a strong dose of reality. Her jaw dropped when she heard her mentor's reply.

"As a matter of fact I have. And I do," said the doctor, her eyes riveted to Rebecca's.

"But how could you? You're a doctor! You have an obligation. Caring is your life; it's who you are!" Rebecca was obviously steamed that this woman whom she'd respected could be so calloused.

"Rebecca, caring is not who I am!" said the doctor in a stern and professional tone. "Caring is what I do. Here, look at this cup." Dr. Anderson filled her teacup right to the top with some water from Rebecca's glass. This water is our caring; it's in us to give. Now pay attention. Is caring what I do, or is it who I am?" She lifted her cup and poured it into her teapot. "There. I've given all the caring I can give today; it's all gone. Now what?"

Rebecca looked a little puzzled. "Now you've done the right thing, you've used your caring and you've helped others," she said in an edgy tone.

"But Rebecca, look at my cup. It's empty. If caring is what I do, then I'm fine. But what if caring is who I am?" Rebecca's fingers began to tingle as she stared at the empty cup. She could hear her heart pumping blood somewhere deep within her chest, her lips began to tremble ever so slightly and her mouth was dry. She lost her words and the feeling of disorientation was creeping over her like it had the last time she'd had a panic attack. Seeing what was happening, Dr. Anderson grabbed Rebecca by the hand and spoke firmly. "Stay with me now. What do you see?"

"It's empty," was all she could whisper, before the tears took over and she felt the full weight of her words. "It's empty. Just like me." Like surgery, Dr. Anderson knew that often a patient had to be cut deeply, before they would be able to live fully. And this had been a deep cut for her young friend. She picked up the teapot and filled her mug with herbal tea.

"If caring is what I do, I can learn to do it well. When I empty myself out, I put my escape plan into action and I fill my cup again. I exercise, spend time with friends, limit my helping, unplug my phone, eat right, rest, and play. Rebecca smiled a tiny bit as she pulled herself together. Dr. Anderson's advice was starting to sound a lot like Dexter's life priorities. "Rebecca listen to me. If caring is who I am, every time I'm empty, I lose my identity. I lose me. If helping is who I am, every time I'm empty, I disappear. It's like I'm lost and I can't know where I am again until I'm helping someone. That kind of living leads to anger, and frustration, and anxiety, and helping others because I need to feel good about me. Is that what you want?"

Her words felt like a cold, hard slap in the face. There was nothing more vile to Rebecca than helping someone else, just to feel good about yourself. Helping should never be selfish. Her reaction was instant and it was strong. "No! That's not what I want. But I feel trapped. How can I change? What can I do? I don't want to be an empty cup? I don't want to hurt people. I want to be good at caring, but . . ." Rebecca's voice trailed off as she stared out the window, wiping tears from her eyes. She continued in a whisper, "but not like this. How can I change?"

Dr. Anderson sat up straight and put on her best educator's voice. Finally, Rebecca had asked the right question. "You do exactly what I did. You learn. You pay attention. You do your homework. You figure out what you need. You make some changes. And you make up your mind right here and right now that you're re-entering the world of mere mortals. No more superhero cape. Will you do it?"

Rebecca watched the tea floating in the mug and thought for a moment about life without a cape. Dr. Anderson was right. When she was caring for others she felt complete, like she was doing the very thing she was made to do. But when she had no one to care for, she felt out of place, empty, and lost.

As she thought about the cape and tried to convince herself that she wasn't all that bad, her mind took her back to early Tuesday morning. Monday had been one of the hardest days of her life and Monday night she'd had a panic attack. But when she woke up early Tuesday morning, instead of paying attention to her own need for rest, she'd immediately started thinking about how she would help her friends. Instead of taking a few days to rest, she'd agreed to listen to Shae and, instead of helping, she'd hurt a friend. And then there was Amy. Instead of recognizing that her friend was making poor choices, she'd blamed herself for Amy's decisions. Zach's fight with Clifton was her fault too, because she couldn't break through a mob and stop it. She'd even blamed herself for Alisa's pregnancy. Now that she thought about it, the idea seemed funny. How could Alisa's pregnancy be her fault? It was crazy, but over the last few days she'd believed it all and she'd made every problem her fault. She could hear her cape now, snapping crisply in the wind. It was painfully obvious; she needed to make some changes before things got any worse. Rebecca looked at Dr. Anderson who sat waiting for her reply, "Yeah, I guess I can give it a try," she finally responded in a sad and uncommitted voice.

But her mentor wasn't interested in half-hearted commitments.

"That's not good enough Rebecca."

"What do you mean?" she said, more than a little surprised at the doctor's response. "This isn't exactly easy for me. Do you have any idea how hard this is?" she said throwing her hands up into the air for emphasis.

Dr. Anderson smiled. "If you only knew," she said under her breath. "No pain, no gain. This isn't something you try on like a new pair of shoes. It's yes, or it's no. Now which is it?" It was hard to stand firm, but there would be no change without a clear commitment to the process.

"Yes, alright then. No more cape!" Rebecca said firmly in a tone that registered irritation and surrender. "You're worse than Ms. Crandle!"

"Indeed I am. Now, let's get that escape plan finished so you'll know how to re-fill when your caregiving drains you." Dr. Anderson paused and smiled a wide, silly grin. "It'll be fun," she said. But Rebecca wasn't altogether pleased. How would she ever learn to draw the line between her friends' choices and her own helping? How would she learn to live a cape-less life? What would life look like if she started paying attention to filling her own cup? It all sounded so selfish.

"Fun? Did you say, 'it'll be fun'?" Rebecca said, rolling her eyes and groaning in pain. "Has anyone ever told you that you have a twisted sense of humour?"

~ 15 TUCK ~

Zach pushed the apartment door open, glad that it was Friday and that he'd gotten through one of the hardest weeks of his life. As he stepped from the hall into the tiny apartment, he found himself standing face to face with Grandpa Turner, or Tuck as the kids had always called him. "What are you doing here?" Zach said with a smile as he walked into a large embrace. With the seriousness of her son's injury, Zach's mom had been calling family members since Tuesday morning to let them know what had happened. She'd called to speak with her ex, but the new girlfriend had told her that he'd been gone since Monday afternoon. She didn't know much, just that a few friends had dropped in and convinced him to drive to Toronto to make some kind of delivery. She had no idea how to get in touch with him, or when he'd be home. But when Tuck had received her call, he'd jumped in the car and headed for Winnipeg without a moment's hesitation. He was retired now and, since grandma had died of cancer two years ago, he'd been living in their big farm house all alone. Zach's mom had told him that he didn't need to bother, but Tuck had insisted on dropping everything and coming to spend a few days with them.

"It's good to see you, son," Tuck said as he squeezed his grandson with the strength of a man half his age. Even though he looked old and weather-beaten, his arms were still solid. He was tall enough to have to duck his head when he walked through a doorway and his hands looked like they could wrap half way around a basketball. But Grandpa Tuck had always been a gentle giant and he'd treated Zach and Clifton like they were his own boys.

106

"I hear you've had a difficult few days," he said as they each found a seat near Zach's mom.

"Yeah, I guess you could say that. Let's see, we had a visit from your idiot son, Clifton got paralyzed, the police tossed me in jail and then tried to charge me with attempted murder. I'd call that a difficult few days." Zach wasn't looking for a fight; he liked his grandpa. As a matter of fact, this had been the only man he'd ever respected and he felt completely comfortable being frank with him.

Tuck chuckled a little, "My idiot son, huh? Well, I suppose that's not too far from the truth," he said, shaking his gray head and rubbing the back of his neck. Noticing that his grandson was looking like a young man, Tuck felt disappointed that he hadn't made more of an effort to visit. The last time they'd shared a hug it had been to say goodbye after the custody hearings and that had been almost a year. As he sat staring at his grandson, Tuck's mind wandered; had it been a year already? "Look how you've grown, Zach. And listen to you calling your father an idiot. He may not be the best father, but that's some pretty strong language, don't you think?"

"Not strong enough," Zach said, as he stretched his legs out and set them up on the coffee table. "Do you know he came to visit us on Monday morning? He knows he's not supposed to be here, but he comes barging in just like he owns the place. He is an idiot, just like Clifton."

Zach's mom jumped in to correct her son, "Let's be careful with our words. Your father's not an idiot and neither is Clifton. They just have some things they need to work out."

"Yeah, just a few minor issues Mom, like assault, constant drinking, and insanity. Nothing a few decades in a mental hospital won't solve." Zach rose from his chair and walked to the kitchen to grab a drink. Looking back toward the living room, he noticed that both his mom and his grandfather were sitting in silence, staring at him. "What? What did I do?"

"Zach, come sit by me. There's something I need to talk to you about." With drink in hand, his grandson returned to his chair across from the old man and neither of them spoke for the longest time. After drawing a heavy breath, Tuck finally broke the ice.

"Zach, my daddy was a preacher and he never allowed strong drink in his house, but I didn't care much when I was young. I didn't know it was strange not to drink until the guys from the fire hall started teasing me about it after a shift one night." Tuck settled into the couch like he was preparing for one of his life-adventure stories that Zach had come to love. "They'd always invite me to the local watering hole after our shift and one day, well, I gave in and decided to go with them. I watched them throw back their beers and then, when they were too drunk to drive, I'd take them all home. Early one morning, a call came into the fire hall waking us up right out of a sound sleep. It was a big house blaze across town and, within minutes, we were suited up and in the truck ready to go. But somehow during the night, the battery in truck number one had died. We had to get the captain's car to give her a boost. We could hardly sit still waiting for that truck to start." Tuck shifted uncomfortably as the memories came to life behind his aging eyes. "That house burned to the ground, Zach, and by the time we got to the site, there wasn't much fire-fightin' left to do." He paused for a moment, searching the ground for a way to get the rest of his story out. Zach watched him closely, not sure why Tuck wanted him to hear this story. "I found a little girl in the house that morning, Zach. She'd been burned real bad in the fire. She died. After we got back to the station, the captain started piecing things together. It had been my job to clean the front seat of the truck the night before and I'd left the interior light on. The battery was dead and, because of my carelessness, so were a mother and her little girl." Tuck glanced out the apartment window for a moment and Zach turned to look at his mom for some explanation from her. She looked down at her feet, unable to hold her son's gaze.

"Tuck, why are you telling me all this now?"

His grandpa cleared his throat. "Son, when I heard that Clifton was in a coma, I knew I'd waited too long. I don't want to miss my chance with you, Zach. I know it doesn't make sense right now but just let me finish."

"Alright," Zach said as he leaned forward, his elbows gently resting on his knees.

"After that fire, things started to change for me. Things I won't go into right now, but you might say I was coming unraveled at the seams. I had nightmares, bad ones. And I felt sad all the time, sad enough to want to die for what I'd done. I started drinking with the boys after our shifts and, soon enough, I was in there every night drinking all by myself. I got to be quite a drunk. I often came home after my shifts looking for some way to unload my anger."

Zach couldn't believe what he was hearing and felt sick about where the conversation was going. "What do you mean you came home to unload your anger?" Tuck gave his daughter-in-law a quick glance and then turned his attention back to Zach. "Sometimes I'd yell and lots of times I'd get mad for little things like a shoe on the floor or a broken dish in the garbage. But I was losing control, and one night I hit your grandma. Your dad didn't take kindly to it and before we knew it, we found ourselves fighting."

"My dad fought you trying to protect grandma?" Zach was stunned and, for just a moment, it felt like he was spinning, his entire understanding of his world and his life radically altered with one little piece of information.

"That's right. He hated my drinking and for years I'd come home looking for a fight and he was more than happy to give me one. Sometimes we just threw words but, most of the time, it was our fists." Tuck paused again to catch his breath. It was an embarrassing story, one he'd hoped Zach would never hear. After a few moments, he continued, "I don't know how long I've got to live, Zach, but I wanted you to know the truth. I wanted you to know that it was my fault your dad ended up a drunk and it was my fault he ruined your life. I may never get the chance to ask Clifton, but I can ask you and your mom." Tuck looked tired and Zach noticed that he seemed to be leaning over more than usual, like he was carrying a load of rocks on his back. "Zach, Teresa, I'm sorry for what I did to your life. I'll understand it if you never want to speak to me again, but I'm hear to say that I'm sorry and to ask you to forgive me. And I know it sounds crazy Zach, but now that you know the truth, I'd like you to think about forgiving your dad, too."

Earlier in the week, Zach had crossed a deep river as he sat in Mr. Hiebert's class talking about peace. In that moment, he'd wanted peace more than anything, but now listening to his grandfather's story, he realized old habits die hard. He had no intention of giving in to peace. "You were a drunk?" he said, with an angry edge to his voice.

But Tuck didn't respond. He'd expected Zach to be upset, and it was time to sit and let him vent.

Standing to his feet, Zach's voice got louder, "You beat my grandma and my dad?" Zach was pacing the room and throwing out questions as he dealt with the shock of this new information. "And now you want me to forgive him for what he's done to us?" Zach laughed, "You've got to be kidding! I'll never forgive that pig for what he's done to me!" As his anger gained momentum, Zach's confidence increased and he pointed a finger at Tuck, "You're just like him. You come here asking me to forgive you and to forgive him. Let me ask you this: Who have you ever had to forgive? Your father loved you; he didn't even drink. Give me a break! You don't have any idea what it's like to be filled with hatred. It's just not that easy to forgive and forget."

Tuck hung his head in shame, wishing that he could turn back the clock to live his life again. He sighed deeply, not able to meet Zach's angry eyes and very slowly, he lifted his enormous hands and placed them over his face. When he finally dropped his hands into his lap, Zach could tell that Grandpa Tuck had been crying. Not deep sobs, but the kind of tears a warrior might cry leaning over a fallen friend on the battlefield. He was strong and quiet, and terribly sorry for the lives he had destroyed.

Zach was floored. He'd never seen his grandpa cry and it was more than just a little unnerving. After a few moments, Tuck took a kleenex from Zach's mom and when he could finally speak, his words were soft and full of emotion. "Zach, you're right. I never had to forgive my dad. I was the monster who hurt my little boy and I was the one who taught him everything he's used to ruin your life. But I understand hatred son, just like you do. The only difference is, I hated myself. And I can tell you that the hardest person to forgive is not the one who breaks your heart, Zach; it's yourself. When I stopped drinking, I realized that my choices had destroyed other people's lives, like yours and your moms, and the only thing I could think of doing was to take my own life. I thought about it pretty serious, but it dawned on me that I owed you and your mom somethin' better. I've started going to my Alcoholics Anonymous meetings again. I'm moving through the twelve steps and one of them is to apologize for the things I've done to hurt people. I didn't come here to push you to forgive your dad, that's something we can talk about later. For now son, I'm asking you to forgive me for what my actions have done to your life."

Zach was completely disarmed. He'd never heard any man talk like this before, not ever. As he stood watching this man he'd loved all his life, the only man he'd ever had any kind of fatherly relationship with, Zach could feel his anger melting away. He sat down slowly beside Tuck, a little shocked that he'd mentioned suicide.

"Gramps," Zach said, "What kept you from doing it, I mean, how come you're still alive?"

Tuck thought about his question for a moment, not sure how much more honesty Zach could take. "I guess I've made peace with my maker son," said the old man, "and now it's time to start making peace with the parts of the world I've messed up. I want to make a few things right and I can't do that if I'm six feet under pushin' up daisies now, can I?"

Zach smiled for what felt like the first time in ages as he reached up with both hands to push the hair back out of his eyes. This was crazy. His grandfather, whom he loved, had taught his father, whom he hated, how to hurt his family. And now he wants me to forgive him? He stared at his gramps long and hard and couldn't think of anything he'd rather do right at that moment. His mom watched with tears in her eyes as her son did something that set him a world apart from his dad. Reaching over, he put a hand on the old man's shoulder and looked him straight in his eyes. "I forgive you, Tuck," he said as they sat in the healing silence of compassion, "but don't ever ask me to forgive my dad. He's never been sorry for anything he's ever done to me."

Tuck stood and pulled his grandson tenderly to himself and with tears in their eyes they held on to each other. "I'm sorry Zach. I'm so sorry I did this to your life," he said with sincerity. "Thank you for your forgiveness. You have no idea how much this means to me," Tuck said as he wiped his eyes again. "Don't you worry about forgiving your dad right now son, that's a step you'll come to. There's other things we need to talk about first. I'm gonna help you, both of you. We'll get through this together," he said as he held the boy's head tenderly in his large hands.

Zach's mom had been sitting on the couch gently weeping and admiring these two men whom she loved with everything in her. Now she stood and joined them and together they held on and felt, perhaps for the very first time, the safety and love that can only come from family.

~ 16 SWEET REUNION ~

Right after breakfast, Rebecca and Dr. Anderson had gone to the student services office at MacDonald to speak with a crisis counselor about Amy's secret. After the beating Rebecca had taken at the restaurant, she was convinced that this was the right thing to do. Even so, it still felt like she was breaking a confidence. "It's all part of losing the cape," Dr. Anderson had said. "No more superwoman. No more secrets. Trust me. You're going to love your new life!"

By 9:00, she was off to her first class, a little nervous that she might run into an angry Amy in the hallway. I wish I had a couch to hide behind, she thought to herself, as she pictured Dexter's favourite hiding spot. But it wasn't the truth. Rebecca didn't want to hide from Amy. Exactly the opposite was true. Sure, she was afraid Amy would think she betrayed her, but this was life and death. What else could she do?

Sitting down at her usual spot in the cafeteria, Rebecca pulled her lunch from her backpack. She laid her novel open on the top of the table and, within seconds, found herself deaf to the noise around her and totally engrossed in the story. It startled her when someone spoke.

"Hey. Is anybody sitting here?"

At the sound of the girl's voice, she was sure that her heart missed at least one beat. Looking up from her book, she smiled and tried not to overreact.

"No, it's all yours," she said with a hesitant smile. Amy fished her lunch out of her backpack and slowly sat down across from Rebecca. They'd known each other for so long but, right at that moment, they both felt like insecure freshmen on the first day of school. "How 'ya been?" Rebecca asked after a few moments of terribly awkward silence.

"I got called to the office this morning," Amy said, not taking her eyes from Rebecca's.

"Amy, I never meant . . . "

"Rebecca," Amy paused, searching for the right words to finish her sentence, "it's alright. I've been pretty mad all morning, but I guess I would have done the same thing for you." Rebecca smiled and reached across to touch Amy's hand.

"Amy, it was so hard to talk to the school counselor. I felt like a little kid, tattling on her sister, but I didn't know what else to do." Rebecca took a deep breath feeling the tension in the air. "But it was the right thing to do and I'm not sorry I did it. I'd do anything to keep you from killing yourself."

Amy looked out the window and breathed a tiny sigh of relief. It felt good to know that someone on the planet understood her and she was starting to wonder if her reaction to the Calgary move might have been a little extreme.

"The counselor wanted my pills," she said. "I'm not sure why I did it, but I gave them to her. I guess that kinda wrecks my plans, huh." Amy sounded sad about her foiled plan, but it was all Rebecca could do to keep herself from jumping across the table and throwing her arms around her friend. They both knew they'd still have to deal with the move, but at least they'd weathered the immediate crisis.

"I think that's the best news I've ever heard," Rebecca said, wiping the tears from her eyes and grinning ear to ear.

"You're such a cry baby," Amy said, shaking her head in mock disgust as she reached into her pack for kleenex. "Here," she said passing a small plastic package across the table.

"Thanks," Rebecca said, dabbing her eyes and cheeks.

"We should get going. Now that my plans have changed, I've got some homework to finish by Monday. I don't want to waste a whole weekend sitting at my computer." As Amy stood, preparing her pack to leave, something suddenly dawned on Rebecca.

"Amy, wait!" she said, reaching over to grab a hold of her friend's sleeve. "I've got something for you." Rebecca reached into the outside pocket of her backpack and lifted a small yellow box from the zippered pouch. Carefully placing it on the table between them, she removed the lid and lifted the delicate gold chain from the puff of white cotton, and placed it in the center of Amy's palm. Folding Amy's fingers around the treasure, Rebecca looked her friend in the eye. "I know that thoughts about suicide don't just go away. I'm here for you if you need to talk." Up to that point, Amy had been the strong one, but with the gold chain in her hand, surrounded by her friend's touch, Amy felt her own tears streaming from her eyes.

"You're right, Rebecca" she said, holding the heirloom tightly in her warm hand. "I guess I can't promise I'll never think about it again, but it's good to know I'm not alone." Rebecca handed the kleenex package back to her friend and stood to leave.

"You're such a cry baby," she said with a playful smile.

"Whatever," Amy said, as she pulled herself together. As they headed into the hall and prepared to head off in separate directions, Amy called back over her shoulder, "Will I see you at the dance tonight?"

"Yeah, I'll be there with Zach," Rebecca said loud enough to make her blush as she turned and headed up the hallway. Her face was beaming and her steps were light. Her best friend was going to live! How great was that!

~ 17 TAKING THE RISK ~

When the final buzzer closed the school day, Rebecca found herself standing in front of the doors that led to the parking lot. All week she'd been afraid to open these doors, but it was something she knew she needed to do before she left for the weekend. "No pain, no gain," she said under her breath. "If I want to drop my score to 30, I'm going to have to take my life back, and that means I can't be afraid of a parking lot!" She gave the door a push and walked toward the steps. Lifting her eyes, she stopped and took in the incredibly boring sight of a gravel parking lot and a little patch of grass just off to her right. Students were filing past her and cars were skidding out of the lot with passengers hanging out of vehicle windows, screaming things about Friday nights and the weekend. It was normal and she felt a smile creeping out and over her face. "I can do this," she said loud enough to draw a few strange looks from people leaning against a nearby wall. She noticed the spot where she'd last seen Zach and the little parking fence was right where it had always been, not looking at all sad about what it had done to Clifton. Feeling good about conquering her fears, she started to head for home but, just as she stepped off the school property, she heard a voice calling her name. She turned to see Samantha running toward her.

"Hey Rebecca, I'm so glad I caught you before you left. I really need to talk to you." Rebecca took a moment to ask herself what she wanted and, to her surprise, she recognized that she was tired and that, more than anything, she wanted some time alone before the dance. Dr. Anderson's words suddenly filled her mind, "set some limits" and Rebecca couldn't help but smile. The voice of my new conscience, she thought to herself.

"I'd love to talk with you, Sam. How about we meet for lunch on Monday?"

"No! This can't wait," said Sam. "I really need to talk to somebody, like right now, like it's really important."

Rebecca thought of Dexter's need for a potty break and she was eager to talk with Zach. "Well, I've really only got about 10 minutes," she said. "I'm just on my way home."

"Oh, 10 minutes, like that would be great," Sam said as she stood wringing her hands and smiling like she needed to go to the bathroom. Somewhere in the back of her mind, Rebecca could hear the faint sound of a cape snapping in the wind and slowly she could see the image of a lone tea cup sitting empty in the middle of a restaurant table. It felt so good to be needed by others, but she decided, right in that moment, that she was making a change and that she would act on Dr. Anderson's advice and take a risk.

"You know, on second thought, I think we'd better stick with Monday at lunch. I'd love to talk with you, but I really need to be somewhere. If there's some kind of emergency, I can help you find someone else to talk with. Is this an emergency?" Rebecca asked.

"Ah, no, it's not like, an emergency, I just wanted to, you know, like, talk," said Sam. "It's no big deal, like I'll just go talk to Brian," she said with attitude as she slunk away like a rejected dog.

"Great," said Rebecca choosing not to apologize for her actions and working hard to ignore the snit in Sam's voice. "I'll look for you on Monday. We can talk more then." And with that Rebecca had folded her cape and placed it neatly in a bottom drawer. She knew that she would probably have a hard time leaving that cape alone and that it would take some time before she got used to not hearing it flapping behind her in the wind. After all, superheroes are hard to kill. Before heading for home, Rebecca turned to look one last time at the parking lot where she and Zach had faced the angry mob. "Just wait 'till Dr. Anderson hears that a superhero retired today," she said as a smile crept across her lips. I actually chose 'not' to help someone, she said shaking her head in amazement. What a crazy thing to feel good about.

STUDY GUIDE

In this brief study guide, you'll find a few questions to help you think about your own caring. If you're anything like Rebecca, you might want to take out some paper, or pull up to your computer and write your responses. If you're not into writing, consider using the questions as a guide for a conversation you have with someone who cares about you.

1. In part one, *Caring for Friends in Pain*, we find Rebecca overwhelmed with traumatic pain because of Zach's story of abuse, Amy's talk of suicide, the fight, and Clifton's accident. As you've been caring for others, what stories or experiences have overwhelmed you? (If you're writing things down, go ahead and make a list). Describe what it means to you when you say you feel 'overwhelmed' by someone's pain.

2. In part two, *The Unexpected Cost of Caring*, Rebecca experiences most of the items found on the chart titled, "How Caring for Others Can Affect Your Life." You'll find this chart on the next page. Go back and re-read chapters 8, 9, & 10. As you read, pick out the specific ways that Rebecca's caring might be affecting her (use the chart to help you). Have you ever noticed yourself experiencing similar things? Make a list of the items that you've noticed in your own life. How do you think the items on your list are related to your caregiving?

3. In part two, *The Unexpected Cost of Caring*, it seems that Rebecca is constantly misunderstood by the adults in her life. Ms.

Crandle thinks she's a liar and the therapist thinks she's a rebellious teen with Oppositional Defiance Disorder. Can you relate to Rebecca's experience of feeling misunderstood? How can you help people to understand you when you're feeling overwhelmed by the pain of others? Notice Rebecca's relationship with Dr. Anderson. What do you like about the way Dr. Anderson treats Rebecca? Talking to someone helped Rebecca get through a rough time. Who do you know that you could talk to?

4. In part three, *Change*, Rebecca has to face the reality of a high score on the Compassion Fatigue Test, but the real pain for her comes when she stares into Dr. Anderson's empty cup. Read through chapter 14 again. What was it that made this conversation so difficult for Rebecca? If you had been sitting in Rebecca's seat, what would you have found the most challenging to hear?

5. In chapter 14, Dr. Anderson tells Rebecca not to plan her escape route when her house is on fire. By this she means that Rebecca needs to think about how caregiving will affect her and to make plans for staying healthy, before she helps others in pain. As you think about how caregiving affects you, take some time to think about what you need to do to stay healthy. Think about Dexter's advice (ch. 11), Dr. Anderson's advice (ch. 14) and Rebecca's risk in the final chapter.

If you haven't completed the Compassion Fatigue Test yet, go ahead and complete it now. Take some time to think about the numbers you score and consider having a conversation with someone to help you think things through.

How Caring for Others Can Affect Your Life

The Way You Think	The Way You Feel	The Way You Act
Difficulty Concentrating	Powerlessness	Clingy
Confusion	Anxiety	Impatient
Spaciness	Guilt	Irritable
Loss of Meaning	Anger/rage	Withdrawn
Decreased self-esteem	Survivor Guilt	Moody
Preoccupation with Trauma	Shutdown	Regression
Trauma Imagery	Numbness	Sleep disturbance
Apathy	Fear	Appetite changes
Rigidity	Helplessness	Nightmares
Disorientation	Sadness	Hypervigilance
Whirling Thoughts	Depression	Elevated startle response
Thoughts of self-harm or harming others	Hypersensitivity	Use of negative coping (smoking, alcohol, or addictive behavior)
Self-doubt	Emotional roller coaster	Accident proneness
Perfectionism	Overwhelmed	Losing things
Minimization	Depleted	Self-harm behaviors

Your Spiritual Self	The Way You Relate to Others	The Way Your Body Responds
Questioning the meaning of life Loss of purpose Lack of self-satisfaction Pervasive hopelessness Ennui (loss of joy) Anger at God Questioning of prior religious beliefs	Withdrawn Decreased interest in intimacy or sex Mistrust Isolation from friends Impact on parenting (protectiveness, concern about aggression) Projection of anger or blame Intolerance Loneliness	Shock Sweating Rapid heartbeat Breathing difficulties Aches and pains Dizziness Impaired immune system

Source adapted from "Table 3:1 – The Personal Impact of Secondary Traumatic Stress" in *Compassion Fatigue in the Animal-Care Community* by Charles R. Figley and Robert G. Roop (Washington, DC: Humane Society Press, 2006), pg. 23.

PROFESSIONAL QUALITY OF LIFE SCALE

(Compassion Satisfaction and Fatigue Test)

Helping others puts you in direct contact with other people's lives. As you probably have experienced, your compassion for those you help has both positive and negative aspects. Consider each of the following questions about you and your current caregiving. Select the number on the scale that reflects how frequently you have experienced these characteristics in the last 30 days and write it in the column to your left.

0=Never 1=Rarely 2=A Few Times 3=Somewhat Often 4=Often 5=Very Often

	1. I am happy.
	2. I am preoccupied with more than one person I help.
	3. I get satisfaction from being able to help people.
	4. I feel connected to others.
	5. I jump or am startled by unexpected sounds.

	6. I feel invigorated after working with those I help.
	7. I find it difficult to separate my personal life from my life as a caregiver.
	8. I am losing sleep over traumatic experiences of a person I help.
	9. I think that I might have been "infected" by the traumatic stress of those I help.
	10. I feel trapped by my work as a caregiver.
	11. Because of my helping, I have felt "on edge" about various things.
	12. I like my work as a helper.
	13. I feel depressed as a result of helping people.
	14. I feel as though I am experiencing the trauma of someone I have helped.
	15. I have beliefs that sustain me.
	16. I am pleased with how I am able to keep up with helping techniques and protocols.
	17. I am the person I always wanted to be.
	18. My helping makes me feel satisfied.
	19. Because of my helping, I feel exhausted.
	20. I have happy thoughts and feelings about those I help and how I could help them.

	21. I feel overwhelmed by the amount of people I am expected to help.
	22. I believe I can make a difference through my caregiving.
	23. I avoid certain activities or situations because they remind me of frightening experiences of the people I help.
	24. I am proud of what I can do to help.
	25. As a result of my helping, I have intrusive, frightening thoughts.
	26. I feel "bogged down" by the system.
	27. I have thoughts that I am a "success" as a helper.
	28. I can't recall important parts of my work with trauma victims.
	29. I am a very sensitive person.
	30. I am happy that I chose to help others.

Note: This is not the same test that appears in the book given to Rebecca titled, *Compassion Fatigue in the Animal-Care Community*. This is an updated version created by B. Hudnall Stamm, 1997-2005: http://www.isu.edu/~bhstamm. This form may be freely copied as long as: (a) authors are credited (b) no changes are made (c) it is not sold.

Self-scoring Directions

1. Be certain you respond to all items.

2. On some items the scores need to be reversed. Next to your response write the reverse of that score (i.e. 0=0, 1=5, 2=4, 3=3). Reverse the scores on these 5 items: 1, 4, 15, 17 and 29. Please note that the value 0 is not reversed.

3. Mark the items for scoring:

    a. Put an **X** by the 10 items that form the **Compassion Satisfaction Scale**: 3, 6, 12, 16, 18, 20, 22, 24, 27, 30.

    b. Put a **check** by the 10 items on the **Burnout Scale**: 1, 4, 8, 10, 15, 17, 19, 21, 26, 29.

    c. **Circle** the 10 items on the **Trauma/Compassion Fatigue Scale**: 2, 5, 7, 9, 11, 13, 14, 23, 25, 28.

4. Add the numbers you wrote next to the items for each set of items and compare with the theoretical scores.

Disclaimer

The Professional Quality of Life Scale: Compassion Satisfaction and Fatigue Test is presented for educational purposes only. It is not a substitute for informed medical advice or training. Do not use this information to diagnose or treat a health problem without consulting a qualified health or mental health care provider. If you have concerns, contact your health care provider, mental health professional, or your community health center.

Understanding Your Scores

Based on your responses, your personal scores are below. If you have any concerns, you should discuss them with a physical or mental health care professional.

Compassion Satisfaction _____

Compassion satisfaction is about the pleasure you get from being able to help people. Higher scores on this scale represent a greater satisfaction related to your ability to be an effective caregiver. The average score is 37. About 25% of people score higher than 42 and about 25% of people score below 33. If you are in the higher range, you probably derive a good deal of satisfaction from helping others. If your scores are below 33, you may either find problems with your helping, or there may be some other reason—for example, you might derive your satisfaction from activities other than your caregiving.

Burnout _____

Most people have an intuitive idea of what burnout is. Burnout is associated with feelings of hopelessness and difficulties in dealing with caregiving or in helping effectively. These negative feelings usually take some time to occur. They can reflect the feeling that your efforts make no difference, or they can be associated with too many people to care for or an environment that is not supportive to your caregiving. Higher scores on this scale mean that you are at higher risk for burnout.

The average score on the burnout scale is 22. About 25% of people score above 27 and about 25% of people score below 18. If your score is below 18, this probably reflects positive feelings about your ability to be effective in your helping. If you score above 27 you may wish to think about what in your caregiving might make you feel like you're not effective. Your score may reflect your mood; perhaps you were having a "bad day" or are in need of some time off. If the high score persists, or if it is reflective of other worries, it may be a cause for concern.

Compassion Fatigue/Secondary Trauma_____

Compassion fatigue (CF), also called secondary trauma (STS) and related to Vicarious Trauma (VT), is about your caregiving, secondary exposure to extremely stressful events. For example, you may repeatedly hear stories about the traumatic things that happen to other people, commonly called VT. For specific symptoms of CF/STS see "How Caring for Others Can Affect Your Life."

The average score on this scale is 13. About 25% of people score below 8 and about 25% of people score above 17. If your score is above 17, you may want to look closely at "How Caring for Others Can Affect Your Life." While higher scores do not mean that you have a problem, they are an indication that you may want to examine how you feel about your caregiving. You may want to discuss your score with a health care professional.

Reference List

Figley, Charles R. and Robert G. Roop (2006). *Compassion Fatigue in the Animal-Care Community*. Washington, DC: Humane Society Press, 2006.

Lerner, Mark D. (2006). *It's OK Not to Be OK . . . Right Now: How to Live Through a Traumatic Experience.* New York, NY: Mark Lerner Associates.

Saakvitne, K.W., Pearlman, L.A. and the Staff of the Traumatic Stress Institute (1996). *Transforming the Pain: A Workbook on Vicarious Traumatization.* New York, NY: W.W. Norton.

Applied Suicide Intervention Skills Training information available online at: www.LivingWorks.com

The Sidran Institute information available online at: www.Sidran.org/

The American Academy of Experts in Traumatic Stress information available online at: www.aaets.com

Printed in the United States
131392LV00002B/2/P

9 781432 729493